He had the look of a man who could turn a woman inside out, and Kaitlyn's stomach fluttered with awareness when their gazes met

A dozen images flitted through her head. His blue eyes staring intently into hers. His deep voice commanding her not to panic as she clung to the edge of the cliff. His calloused hands moving skillfully over her bare skin to warm her up.

"Kaitlyn...are you up to answering a few questions?"

The sound of her name on his lips sent another shiver up her spine. "You sound like a cop."

He shrugged. "I'm just curious as to what you were doing out in the middle of nowhere alone in a rainstorm."

"I can't remember what happened after the storm hit," Kaitlyn muttered. "I only have a vague recollection of the rescue. If you hadn't come along when you did..."

"Actually, we were already out there searching for fugitives when we got the call that a woman was missing..."

Kaitlyn frowned. "But...you said you're not a cop."

"I'm not." His gaze met hers. "I'm a bounty hunter."

Dear Harlequin Intrigue Reader,

Summer's winding down, but Harlequin Intrigue is as hot as ever with six spine-tingling reads for you this month!

* Our new BIG SKY BOUNTY HUNTERS promotion debuts with Amanda Stevens's *Going to Extremes*. In the coming months, look for more titles from Jessica Andersen, Cassie Miles and Julie Miller.

* We have some great miniseries for you. Rita Herron is back with *Mysterious Circumstances*, the latest in her NIGHTHAWK ISLAND series. Mallory Kane's *Seeking Asylum* is the third book in her ULTIMATE AGENTS series. And Sylvie Kurtz has another tale in THE SEEKERS series— *Eye of a Hunter.*

* No month would be complete without a chilling gothic romance. This month's ECLIPSE title is Debra Webb's *Urban Sensation.*

* Jan Hambright, a fabulous new author, makes her debut with *Relentless.* Sparks fly when a feisty repo agent repossesses a BMW with an ex-homicide detective in the trunk!

Don't miss a single book this month and every month!

Sincerely,

Denise O'Sullivan
Senior Editor
Harlequin Intrigue

GOING TO EXTREMES
AMANDA STEVENS

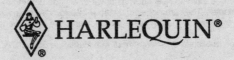

HARLEQUIN®

TORONTO • NEW YORK • LONDON
AMSTERDAM • PARIS • SYDNEY • HAMBURG
STOCKHOLM • ATHENS • TOKYO • MILAN • MADRID
PRAGUE • WARSAW • BUDAPEST • AUCKLAND

Special thanks and acknowledgment are given
to Amanda Stevens for her contribution to
the BIG SKY BOUNTY HUNTER series.

ISBN 0-373-88636-5

GOING TO EXTREMES

www.eHarlequin.com

Printed in U.S.A.

ABOUT THE AUTHOR

Amanda Stevens is the bestselling author of over thirty novels of romantic suspense. In addition to being a Romance Writers of America RITA® Award finalist, she is also the recipient of awards in Career Achievement in Romantic/Mystery and Career Achievement in Romantic/Suspense from *Romantic Times* magazine. She currently resides in Texas. To find out more about past, present and future projects, please visit her Web site at www.amandastevens.com.

CAST OF CHARACTERS

Kaitlyn Wilson—An ambitious reporter who unwittingly stumbles upon the story of a lifetime.

Aidan Campbell—An adrenaline junkie with a savior complex.

Colonel Cameron Murphy—He intends to get Boone Fowler by using any means necessary.

Boone Fowler—An escaped convict who has a new boss...and a new agenda.

Dr. Phillip Becker—His bedside manner could use some work.

Eden McClain—Kaitlyn's childhood friend has important connections and her own ambitions.

Allen Cudlow—A rival reporter with a chip on his shoulder.

Governor Peter Gilbert—A charming man with big plans for his political future.

Prince Nicholai Petrov—Rebuking his father on a world stage has turned him into a rock star.

Big Sky Bounty Hunters—Their search for the fugitives leads them back into the world of international intrigue.

Prologue

It was done.

He'd killed the woman and buried her body in a shallow grave in the Montana wilderness. The wolverines would be at her soon enough, and then the vultures. By the time her body was discovered by some errant backpacker or trapper, her face would be gone, and if luck held, her fingerprints.

A DNA analysis would be required for a positive identification, and that could take days...sometimes weeks in this part of the world. Even if the authorities were able to trace her to the Montana Militia for a Free America, it would be too late. She could not tell them anything now.

Jenny Peltier had paid the ultimate price

*for her betrayal, and as Boone Fowler fol-
lowed the stream through the woods back to
his encampment, he felt no elation or re-
morse at what he'd done. He didn't particularly enjoy killing, although he was good at
it.*

In war, people died. It was as simple as that.

*And they were at war. A war to take back
the country from the corrupt bureaucrats
who contaminated the American way of life
as surely as the pathetic junkies who infested
the American street.*

*They would all be dealt with in time, those
soft, greedy ingrates who knew not the mean-
ing of honor and sacrifice. They would have
to learn the hard way.*

*The bombing of a government building by
the MMFAFA had shocked the nation, but
that would be only one of the many "shots"
that would soon be heard around the world.*

*The day of deliverance had dawned over
Montana, and the winds of liberty would
sweep down in triumph across the prairie
states and march, like Sherman's army,
through the South, conquering nearly sixty
years of malaise, apathy and moral decay.*

The avenging angel of freedom would stand victorious on the squalid doorsteps of the eastern cities and level, in God-like fury, the modern-day Sodom and Gomorrah to the West.

Fowler drew a deep, quivering breath. No matter how many times he delivered that sermon to the faithful, the message never failed to stir him. He had a gift and he knew how to use it. His mother used to say that when he spoke with such passion, he could make people follow him to the ends of the earth. He was counting on that.

Pausing, he knelt at the edge of the stream to wash the blade of the hunting knife he'd used to slit the woman's throat, and then he scrubbed his hands, even though they were already clean. His soul was clean, too. Virtuous.

He was so caught up in the righteousness of his mission that he almost missed the telltale rustle of dead leaves upstream and to his right. The sound was slight, a mere whisper in the wind, but it sent a chill up his spine just the same.

And then Fowler realized that he'd been vaguely uneasy for the last quarter of a mile or so. Even though his mind was preoccupied, his instincts had been warning him of danger.

He should have listened. Whoever was behind him had managed to get the jump on him, so that meant that the tracker was good. A professional. Someone who knew the Montana wilderness as well as Fowler.

He continued to rinse the knife as his senses came fully alert and his mind raced with possibilities. He had a semiautomatic tucked in his belt, but he'd have to wait for the right moment to draw it. A sudden move and the tracker might open fire on him.

From the corner of his eye, he scouted the terrain. When the sound came again, still to his right, Fowler pulled his gun and began firing in that direction as he simultaneously rolled to his left. Seeking cover behind a boulder, he unloaded his weapon without pause and then grabbed a fresh cartridge.

"Drop the weapon!"

Fowler froze. The voice hadn't come from his right at all. Instead, the tracker was downstream and to his left. He'd circled his quarry and now he had Fowler trapped. The rustle of leaves had been a diversion. Pebbles tossed over his head perhaps. A trick as old as time itself, and Fowler had fallen for it.

It wasn't like him to be so careless. While his guard had been down, the man who hunted him had moved in surprisingly close. So close Fowler could practically feel the bastard breathing down his neck.

"Drop the weapon or I'll put a bullet through your brain." The voice was deep, fearless, commanding. A man used to barking orders and having them obeyed.

To prove his point, he fired off a round, blasting to kingdom come a pinecone that had fallen not ten feet from where Fowler hunkered.

Fowler threw down his weapon.

The man came out of the woods then, a tall, powerfully built warrior with the darkest gaze Fowler had ever looked into. He'd killed before. It was there in his eyes. In the steadiness of his hand on his weapon. He'd kill again, too, if he had to. Without hesitation.

He was a military man. His bearing gave him away, and his tracking skills suggested someone with a Special Forces background.

"Who are you?" Fowler asked. "What do you want?"

"I want justice, you son of a bitch." As he walked toward Fowler, rage contorted the man's features, and in the split second it took for him to get his emotions under control, Fowler whipped the pistol out of his ankle holster and fired.

The punch of the bullet knocked the man backward, and he fell with a hard thud to the ground.

A clean shot, right through the heart.

His muscles began to twitch, and Fowler walked over to put another bullet in his head to finish him off. Kicking the man's weapon aside, he lifted his own gun and took aim.

"For the Cause!" he cried in triumph.

Montana State Penitentiary
Monday, 0400 hours

BOONE FOWLER CAME AWAKE slowly. For a moment, he thought he was back in the Montana wilderness, facing off against an old nemesis, but as his mind began to clear, he realized that it had been nothing more than a dream. A recurring nightmare of being hunted. The scenery and the enemy sometimes changed, but the outcome was always the same. It was he who stood victorious under a clear Montana sky—not the hunter.

In reality, it hadn't gone down that way, and now Fowler found himself confined to a six-by-eight prison cell. As he swung his legs over the cot and sat, head in hands, everything came rushing back to him. His capture. The trial. The past five years of his life spent in a hell-hole called the Fortress. A maximum-security prison from which no one had ever escaped.

And all because of a man named Cameron Murphy.

While Fowler had rotted in prison for the past half decade, Murphy had recruited what was left of a Special Forces team he'd once commanded and turned them into the most successful bounty-hunter organization in the country. Although Murphy was the only one Fowler had met face-to-face, he'd made a point of finding out the other men's names. He knew their backgrounds, their specialties, what made them tick.

But it was Murphy alone that Fowler still

saw in his nightmares at night. Murphy's face he saw when he'd beat another inmate almost beyond recognition.

His hatred of Cameron Murphy had helped him survive nearly nine months of solitary confinement in the Dungeon, and his thirst for revenge had kept his rage in check when he'd been placed back into the general population of the prison.

He'd kept his nose clean all these years because he had a plan, and for that, he needed his friends, contacts with the outside world. He needed money for bribes and favors he could call in. He needed all the help he could muster in order to accomplish what had never been done before: escape from the Fortress.

And thanks to a generous benefactor with an ambitious agenda, the moment was finally at hand. Tonight, at lights out, he would instigate a riot, the likes of which the prison guards had never before seen. During the pandemonium, Fowler and his compatriots would be led off to the Dungeon, where they would lay low until the plan could be set in motion.

If all went well, they would soon be free men.

And Cameron Murphy would soon be a dead one.

God help anyone who got in the way.

"For the Cause!" Fowler whispered as adrenaline surged through his veins.

Chapter One

Tuesday, 1400 hours

"Ken, you're breaking up! I can barely hear you!" Pressing the cell phone to her ear, Kaitlyn Wilson tried not to panic. Rain beat like a war drum on the roof of her SUV as she slowly made her way west on Route 9. She'd turned the windshield wipers on high speed, but she still couldn't see a damn thing. "Are you still there?" she asked desperately.

"Major flooding…highway closed…"

Static crackled in Kaitlyn's ear. "Should I turn back? *Dammit!*" The phone went dead and she swore again as she frantically tried to call her boss back. But it was no use. She'd lost the signal.

Okay, situation not good, she summarized

as she tossed the cell phone onto the seat and clutched the steering wheel with both hands.

Since she'd set out for the prison less than an hour earlier, Route 9 had been transformed into a lake. Kaitlyn could no longer even see the pavement. It was only by instinct and sheer dumb luck that she hadn't yet driven off the road.

She could feel the swirling water sucking at the tires as she slowed the vehicle to a crawl, trying to decide what to do. Keep going…or turn back?

Did she really have a choice?

With near-zero visibility, turning the vehicle around without sliding into a ditch would be no easy feat, and besides, she had no way of judging whether the road conditions behind her were any better.

She was in the notorious dead zone on Route 9 where cell-phone signals from the nearest tower were blocked by the mountains. And now static had overpowered the radio so that she couldn't even pick up a weather forecast. She was, in effect, cut off from the rest of the world.

And the water continued to rise.

Why, oh why, hadn't she listened to Ken when he'd cautioned her not to start off alone in the downpour?

"Are you crazy?" he'd shouted. "In case you haven't been paying attention, the entire county is under a flash-flood warning."

"I'll be traveling on high ground for most of the way, and Route 9 never floods." And by now Kaitlyn knew her way to the prison with her eyes closed. "If I leave now, I can get to the press conference before the heavy stuff hits."

"Oh, you think? And just what would you call *that?* A drizzle?" Ken had cast a wary glance out his office window, where rain continued to fall steadily from a bleak, gray sky. It had been coming down nonstop all day.

Kaitlyn had breezily waved off his concern. "You worry too much. Besides, if I don't get to the press conference, we'll be scooped by the *Independent Record,* and you know you don't want that," she said, naming a rival paper.

Ken scowled. "I also don't want the Highway Patrol having to fish you out of a ditch somewhere."

At least he was gracious enough not to

point out that it wouldn't be the first time. "I know what I'm doing, Ken."

His patience finally worn down, he sighed. "Okay, at least take someone with you. Let me get Cudlow on the horn—" He had reached for the phone, but Kaitlyn's outraged screech stopped him.

"Cudlow?" She spoke the name with such utter disdain that Ken gave her a disapproving look. Kaitlyn didn't care. There was no way she'd allow Allen Cudlow—the man who had almost single-handedly derailed her career at the paper five years ago—to accompany her to the warden's press conference. No way in *hell.*

Her feud with Cudlow had started long before Ken Mellon had been brought in when the previous editor in chief had finally retired nine months ago. Kaitlyn had been ecstatic at the prospect of new blood at the *Ponderosa Monitor* because she and Cudlow, who was once the golden boy at the *Monitor,* were finally on equal footing.

"If you truly want to avert a tragedy, you'll put down that phone," she'd warned Ken.

He'd run his fingers through his thinning

hair. "Okay, okay. I get it. You and Cudlow hate each other's guts. I don't know why and I don't much care as long as it doesn't interfere with your reporting. A little professional rivalry can be a good thing. Up to a point." He gave her a warning glare over the top of his bifocals. "But don't carry it too far."

She shrugged. "Just keep him out of my way and everything's cool."

"And anyway," Ken continued as if she'd never spoken, "I really can't spare Cudlow this afternoon. If you insist on attending Warden Green's press conference, I'll have to send him to the state capital to cover Petrov's arrival tonight."

Kaitlyn's mouth dropped. "You can't do that! I've been working on the Petrov piece for weeks!"

"Both stories are breaking and you can't be in two places at once."

Kaitlyn hated it when he got all sensible. It usually meant that she was being unreasonable.

"So what's it to be, Kaitlyn? Petrov...or the prison break?"

Decisions, decisions.

Kaitlyn bit her lip as she quickly weighed the possibilities. "Okay, look. If you have to send Cudlow to the airport to cover Petrov's arrival…that's one thing. But don't give him the story. I'm this close to getting an exclusive."

Ken's gaze narrowed. "How close?"

Kaitlyn hesitated. "I've almost got it wrapped up."

Not quite the truth, but thanks to some behind-the-scenes maneuvering by an old friend, Kaitlyn was inching closer to the "get" of a lifetime.

She might be a no-name reporter for a small-time newspaper in Podunk, Montana, but she had what even the network superstars didn't have…an inside track with Nikolai Petrov.

Prince Nikolai Petrov to be exact.

The very sound of his name reminded Kaitlyn just how swoon-worthy the guy was. His good looks alone had melted feminine hearts all over the world, but since his impassioned speech before the United Nations, he'd reached near-rock-star status.

In a dazzling display of charm, integrity

and sheer chutzpah, the crown prince of Lukinburg had implored the world community to step in and remove his own father from power for the sake of his impoverished and war-torn country. Then he'd embarked on a whirlwind tour across the country in an effort to win the hearts and minds of the American people in the event a U.N.-sanctioned, U.S.-led military invasion became necessary to overthrow King Aleksandr.

Each time the prince gave one of his heavily publicized speeches, his father would issue a stinging rebuttal from the safety of his palace in Lukinburg. The bitter family feud was being played out on the world stage, and the stakes couldn't have been higher.

Working his way west, Petrov was due to arrive in Montana later that night as the VIP guest of Governor Peter Gilbert, and as luck would have it, Eden McClain, one of Kaitlyn's oldest and closest friends, just happened to be the governor's personal assistant.

Eden had been an invaluable source since Gilbert's reelection campaign had entered its final weeks, providing Kaitlyn access to the governor's inner circle that even reporters from some of the more prestigious papers in the state were denied.

In return, Kaitlyn tried not to cross boundaries that would strain her and Eden's friendship, but with a Petrov exclusive on the line, she hadn't been able to resist pressuring her friend to use her connections.

Kaitlyn gritted her teeth as she gripped the steering wheel. While she was stuck on Route 9, Allen Cudlow was probably slithering his way to Helena to cover Petrov's arrival at that very moment. And, knowing Cudlow, he would somehow finagle his own interview with Petrov if for no other reason than to spite Kaitlyn.

She would never hear the end of it, either. Cudlow would never let her live down the fact that she'd passed up an exclusive with Prince Petrov in order to cover a prison break from the state penitentiary located a few miles west of Ponderosa.

But this was no ordinary prison break. Not only had the convicts pulled off the impossible—escaping from the Fortress—but they were led by Boone Fowler, the notorious militia member who had masterminded the bombing of a federal building five years ago.

So Kaitlyn had had to make a hard choice… a dangerous terrorist or a real-life Prince Charming.

Some choice.

What were the chances of two such major stories colliding in Montana, of all places? Granted, the state capital routinely had its share of political squabbles and backroom deals, but Ponderosa—Kaitlyn's home base and the town closest to the prison—was normally a snooze fest.

Not so these days with Boone Fowler on the loose.

Ruthless and demented, the man would destroy his own mother if he deemed the sacrifice necessary to advance his glorious "Cause." He had a lot of blood on his hands, including that of Jenny Peltier, who, along with Eden McClain, had been Kaitlyn's best friend all through school.

Not that Kaitlyn's hands were exactly clean in Jenny's death, either, she thought bitterly. She'd used Jenny to further her own agenda just as surely as Boone Fowler had.

Sweet, impressionable Jenny.

She'd come to Kaitlyn for help, and what had Kaitlyn done? Kind and loving friend that she'd been, she'd sent Jenny back into the lion's den. Without regard for her safety. Without regard for anything except getting a story that would make her Pulitzer prize winning father sit up and take notice.

Yes, she had actually been that selfish and that blindly ambitious, so much so that she'd been willing to betray a friend without a second thought.

Kaitlyn wanted to believe that she was a changed person, but she was very much afraid there was a special place in hell reserved for friends like her.

Maybe she would see Boone Fowler there…if not before.

A shiver tingled down her backbone at the prospect of meeting such a monster face-to-face. It was one thing to write about Fowler's criminal exploits from the safety of her cubicle at the paper; quite another to actually confront him. And yet that was what she had sent Jenny to do.

Kaitlyn tried to will away the guilt that

still ate at her after all these years. If she'd learned anything from her mistakes, though, it was that dwelling on the what-ifs and the what-might-have-beens did little good. She needed to concentrate on what she could do to send Fowler back to prison.

Covering the warden's press conference was a start, but unfortunately, the weather refused to cooperate and the situation was becoming extremely dire.

Kaitlyn tensed as water sloshed over the hood of her vehicle, threatening to stall out the engine. She couldn't keep going. The road was virtually impassable.

In her tenure as a reporter, she'd covered the aftermath of flash flooding, but she'd never actually been caught in one herself. Now she knew firsthand just how terrifying it could be.

After squelching her initial panic, she quickly came to the conclusion that her only recourse was to abandon the vehicle and head for high ground.

Stuffing her cell phone and a flashlight into the zippered pocket of her waterproof parka, she opened the door and climbed out.

The floodwaters were already knee-deep and so cold she could hardly catch her breath. She clung to the door for a moment, trying to get her footing as the flowing water threatened to sweep her off balance.

Bracing as best she could, she waded toward the embankment at the shoulder of the road and, using roots, her fingernails, and sheer determination, she climbed her way to safety, then turned to survey her surroundings.

The vista was breathtaking. The highway was almost completely flooded, and the water continued to rise. Her SUV was slowly being swallowed, and as rain beat down on Kaitlyn's face, she tried to figure out what to do. She could make her way along the top of the embankment, staying in sight of the highway, and hope that someone came along. But if the road had been closed, that possibility wasn't too likely.

Her best option was to keep climbing, Kaitlyn decided. At some point, she was bound to get a cell phone signal, and then she could call for help. And if she kept walking, she would eventually reach Eagle Falls, a small logging community seven miles north of the highway.

Striking out alone through the wilderness with dangerous convicts on the loose normally wouldn't have been her first choice, but the prisoners had been on the run for nearly twenty-four hours. It was doubtful they were even still in the area, and besides, Kaitlyn wasn't so sure she'd be any safer sitting on the side of a deserted road. She had no idea how long it would take for the water to go down, and even then, her vehicle would be inoperable. No one would miss her until morning so it was likely she would be sitting there all night. If she wanted to reach Eagle Falls before dark, she'd have to leave now.

Taking one last glance at her submerged vehicle, she squared her shoulders and began to climb.

TWILIGHT FELL early across the mountain, but Kaitlyn resisted the temptation to use her flashlight as she trudged along an old hunting path. She needed to conserve the batteries because, if she didn't reach Eagle Falls soon, her flashlight could very well be the only thing standing between her and the coyotes and mountain lions that prowled the area. Not to mention the grizzlies.

Lions, coyotes, and bears, oh, my, she thought with a nervous laugh. She'd definitely been out in the elements too long.

Ever since she'd left the highway, she hadn't seen one single sign of human life. Even the animals had taken to high ground, and it was as if she was alone in a watery universe. Kaitlyn had never realized how profound complete silence could be, nor had she grasped the vastness of the Montana wilderness. She now had a new appreciation for the frontier men and women who had been able to navigate their way through the mountainous terrain with nothing more than their own keen sense of survival.

Even though she had yet to reach the top of the summit, the ground had leveled off a bit. The going was easier now, but Kaitlyn's spirits had plummeted. She was wet, exhausted and freezing. All she could think about was a hot bath and a warm bed, preferably in that order.

She'd been hiking for the better part of

two hours when she finally saw a glimmer of light through the trees.

Civilization! At last!

Kaitlyn's heart leaped in anticipation.

She stumbled over a tree branch in her excitement and forced herself to slow down. A twisted ankle—or worse, a broken leg—was the last thing she needed.

As she emerged from a thicket of ponderosa pines into a small clearing, she realized the light came from what appeared to be an old hunting lodge.

She scanned the area immediately surrounding the rustic building. There were no utility poles or wires that she could see, and she couldn't hear a generator. Someone had probably lit a lantern. Another stranded motorist perhaps who'd arrived at the lodge before her.

Kaitlyn doubted the cabin was equipped with a phone line, either, but whoever was inside might have a working cell phone or even a short-wave radio. At the very least, they might be able to offer her a warm, safe place to spend the night.

Her first instinct was to rush up the rickety steps and pound on the door as hard as she could until someone answered. But her impulses had already gotten her into trouble once that day. She was alone, unarmed, and too exhausted to put up much of a fight should she need to. Her best bet was to approach the cabin with extreme caution. Do a bit of reconnoitering before she made her presence known.

Slipping across the wet ground, she flattened herself against the log wall and eased toward the window. She could hear voices inside. Loud, angry voices that sent a chill up her spine.

Taking care not to be seen, she inched toward the window and peered in, then jumped back, her heart flailing at what she'd seen.

A half-dozen or so men milled about inside the cabin. They were dressed in fatigues and were armed with what appeared to be automatic weapons, but Kaitlyn didn't think they were soldiers. One of the men stood so near the window that she'd glimpsed a tattoo on the bicep of his left arm beneath his dark green T-shirt.

An upside-down burning American flag…

the symbol used by the Montana Militia for a Free America.

She'd seen that same tattoo on Boone Fowler's arm when he'd proudly displayed it at his trial.

And on Jenny Peltier's arm when she'd come to Kaitlyn for help.

Kaitlyn had stared at the symbol in horror when Jenny had shoved up her sleeve. "Those people are murderers, Jenny. Terrorists! Why would you get involved with a group like that?"

"Because of Chase," Jenny whispered. "I owed him that much."

Jenny's older brother had died in a war she and her family had always considered unjust and illegal. Her stepfather had railed against the government for years, and Chase's death had only added fuel to the fire. Jenny had been so torn up with grief that her stepfather's rants must have colored her perception of what had really happened. But Kaitlyn would never have guessed that she would have taken her hatred so far.

Squeezing her eyes closed, Kaitlyn willed away the memory. Boone Fowler had killed her best friend, but she couldn't afford to lose control now. She had to get out of there before they saw her. She had to find a way to contact the authorities. Fowler and his cohorts were armed and dangerous. It wasn't just her life on the line.

Clutching her cell phone, she prayed that she would be able to get a signal and summon help. But as she started to slip away from the cabin, a scream from inside drew her back to the window.

She tried not to make a sound, but what she saw sent a gasp to her throat. The man nearest the window had moved away so that she had a clear view of the interior. The convicts had taken a hostage. They'd stripped him and bound him to a wooden chair. He was bleeding profusely from his wounds and seemed barely conscious as his head lolled forward, chin on chest.

As Kaitlyn watched in horror, one of the MMFAFA members approached him. Grabbing the man's hair, he pulled back his head, exposing his throat as he slipped a knife blade along the delicate skin, drawing even more blood.

The man groaned and began to babble. He spoke in what sounded to Kaitlyn like German. *"Gotthilife mich. Gotthilfe uns alle, wenn Sie gelingen."* He muttered it over and over. Kaitlyn tried to translate, but her high school German was too long ago and she was so terrified she couldn't think straight. But she could tell from his demeanor that he was begging for mercy.

His pleas fell on deaf ears. Someone shouted, "For the Cause!" and they all took up the chant as the knife whipped across the hostage's throat.

The gush of crimson sent Kaitlyn into a momentary state of shock. She stood paralyzed at the window, hand clapped to her mouth to suppress her own scream. She couldn't move. She hardly dared to breathe. If they saw her…

She must have made an involuntary sound, or perhaps some instinct told him she was there. Boone Fowler had been standing with his back to the window, and now he turned slowly, his gaze meeting Kaitlyn's through the window.

Bloodlust glinted in his eyes.

Kaitlyn had never seen such a cold, demonic expression. His lips twisted cruelly as he acknowledged her presence and then he sprang like a panther across the room to the window.

At that moment, Kaitlyn knew she was a dead woman walking, but her instinct for survival was stronger that she'd ever imagined and, whirling, she sprinted for the woods.

She heard the glass shatter behind her as Fowler leaped through the window, and then the more immediate sound of rustling leaves and snapping twigs underneath his feet as he pursued her.

Kaitlyn ran like the devil himself was behind her. She was young, fit, and had the advantage of fear-induced adrenaline spurring her through the wet twilight. For a moment, she thought she might actually have a chance of getting away, and then she came to a dead stop as she found herself teetering on the brink of a canyon.

She spun, her gaze darting about for another way out, but Fowler had already found her. He was perhaps twenty yards away and closing in on her as he took in her predicament. Then his steps slowed. No need to hurry. He had her cornered.

Kaitlyn's heart pounded as she watched him. Would she be better off to fling herself from the cliff…or wait for Fowler to seal her fate?

"Who are you?" he asked in a voice that gave nothing away of his past. He might have been a fellow traveler that she'd stumbled upon in the woods. Not the remorseless killer who had the blood of two hundred innocents on his hands.

Kaitlyn didn't answer him. Her breath was coming so hard and fast she couldn't speak.

Fowler took a menacing step toward. "I asked you a question, girl. Who are you?"

"Kaitlyn Wilson."

His gaze narrowed. "Do I know you?"

"I'm a reporter for the *Ponderosa Monitor.*"

"A *reporter?*" He took another step toward her. "Who told you where to find me? *Answer me!*"

Kaitlyn jumped at the rage in his voice. "No one. I didn't come up here looking for you. I got stranded in a flash flood on Route 9. I kept walking until I could get a cell-phone signal."

"Who knows you're up here?"

No one, Kaitlyn thought in despair. *Not a single soul.* "The police. I called 9-1-1 for help. They'll be here soon—"

"You're lying. You can't get a cell-phone signal up here for miles." He started toward her again, and Kaitlyn backed away, gasping when she wobbled too close to the edge of the cliff.

Fowler laughed. "Careful. That's a long fall."

He was obviously enjoying himself, like a cat playing with a mouse. Even in the gathering darkness, Kaitlyn could see the gleam in his eyes. The feral grin that made her blood run cold. He was going to kill her as he'd killed Jenny. Maybe it was destiny catching up with her after all these years.

Maybe it was nothing more than her imagination, but Kaitlyn could have sworn she felt Jenny's presence in the wind that swept through her hair. In the rain that fell like teardrops on her face.

Come on, Kaitlyn! You've always been able to think on your feet. You can talk your way out of this if you try.

Kaitlyn tried to beat back her panic as she moistened her lips. "I didn't come up here to find you, but now that I have…I can help you. I can give you a public platform. Arrange for you to tell your side of things—"

Before Fowler could reply, a voice said from the darkness, "I'm afraid we can't allow that."

Kaitlyn couldn't see the newcomer. He remained hidden in the woods behind Fowler, but there was something familiar about his voice. She'd heard it before.

If he knew her, maybe he'd help her somehow…

"Who are you?" she asked, sounding far more desperate and frightened than she would have liked.

"It doesn't matter who I am. You've stumbled upon the story of a lifetime, it seems. I'm sorry you won't live to tell it."

Kaitlyn's stomach churned at his words. "You don't have to do this. I don't even know who you are."

"You'd put it together sooner or later. I truly am sorry, but in times like these, sacrifices have to be made. Our Cause is far too important to risk letting you go."

Oh, God...

"Kill her and make it quick," he said to Fowler. "Have your men dispose of both bodies and make sure they clean up inside."

"Whatever you say. You're calling the shots." *For now,* Fowler's tone implied. "For the Cause!" he shouted in triumph.

"For the Cause," the disembodied voice agreed.

Fowler lifted his weapon, but in the split second before he pulled the trigger, the ground gave way beneath Kaitlyn's feet. Loosened by all the rain, the edge of the canyon broke free and slid downward, carrying Kaitlyn with it.

She screamed as the bullet whizzed past her cheek, and then she plunged backward into nothing but darkness.

Chapter Two

Wednesday, 1600 hours

The storm had let up overnight and the early part of Wednesday morning, but as the afternoon slipped away, a new front moved in, bringing rain bands that slammed across the JetRanger's path. Cruising at an altitude of three hundred feet beneath heavy cloud cover, the chopper rose and fell like a roller coaster as wind gusts of up to twenty-five knots batted it to and fro.

No problem, Aidan Campbell thought as he kept his eyes pealed out the window for the missing woman. The JetRanger III was a reliable machine, and the pilot, Jacob Powell, had nearly twenty years of experience under his belt. Plus, he was trained to fly in thirty-knot and above winds. Aidan had seen the guy navigate through near-hurricane conditions—and while they were taking heavy fire, to boot. Comparatively speaking, this search-and-rescue mission was a piece of cake.

The request for assistance by the county sheriff's office had come into Big Sky Bounty Hunters headquarters at approximately 1300 hours, and Cameron Murphy had immediately notified his teams—already in the field searching for the escaped prisoners—to be on the lookout for a Ponderosa woman whose abandoned and submerged vehicle had been spotted on Route 9. Presumably, she'd taken to high ground during the storm, but the fact that she hadn't been heard from in over twenty-four hours didn't bode well for her safety.

Aidan and Powell had started their search in the area where her vehicle had been seen and then gradually widened the perimeter. It was like looking for the proverbial needle in a haystack. Their only hope was that the woman would somehow be able to signal them when—and if—she heard the engine.

To fight off the strong headwinds, Powell

swerved the chopper's nose and tail back and forth like a scampering sand crab. The maneuver helped, but the altimeter was still going crazy. Nausea tugged at Aidan's stomach as he lifted the binoculars and scanned the scenery below them. They'd flown out of the heavy rain, but visibility was still poor and they were losing the light. He could make out little more than the treetops.

Flying at low altitudes in mountainous terrain was dangerous under the best of conditions, but in bad weather, it was a particular dicey operation. But Aidan knew there was no turning back, for him or for Powell, until they absolutely had to. If the woman was still alive, she might not survive another night in the wilderness.

Aidan didn't say it aloud, but for the past half hour or so, he'd been plagued by the nagging worry that despite their best efforts, they might come up short this time. SAR operations didn't always have happy endings. He knew that better than anyone.

His headset sputtered to life.

"See anything?" Powell asked him.

He shook his head. "Negative."

"*Damn.*" The frustration in Powell's voice mirrored Aidan's concern. Darkness was falling and they were rapidly reaching the point at which the helicopter wouldn't have enough fuel to return to base. A decision would soon have to be made.

He glanced at Powell. "What do you think?"

Powell's mouth was set in a grim line. "One more circle and then we'll have to head in." He turned south, putting the wind at their tail and the JetRanger sprinted forward.

As they passed over a gorge cut deep into the side of the mountain, Aidan pointed out the window. "I've been rock climbing in that canyon. It's at least a hundred-foot drop to the floor."

Powell shrugged. "Devil's Canyon. What of it?"

"If memory serves, there's an old hunting lodge around here somewhere…yeah, just through that break in the trees. See it? It's a long shot, but she could be holed up inside, waiting for the weather to clear."

"I doubt she would have made it up this

far, but hold on," Powell said. "We'll drop down and see if we spot movement."

As he swung around, something twinkled in the deep recesses of the canyon, drawing Aidan's attention. He watched for a moment, thinking it might have been his imagination, but then it came again. A flicker of light.

Couldn't be a campfire in the rain...

"Did you see that?" Aidan pointed excitedly toward the canyon. "I saw a light down there."

Powell executed a one-eighty spin, turning his nose straight into the headwind. The helicopter shuddered, as if a giant hand had smacked it across the hull.

The rim of the canyon was nothing but rocks and marshy ground. If they set down, the chopper was likely to sink in the mud and they'd never get it out. Landing on the floor of the narrow ravine was not an option, either, and a rescue party could take hours to get there.

The light kept blinking. It might have been Aidan's imagination, but the signal seemed more rapid now. More desperate.

"I'll go down and have a look," he shouted into the mouthpiece.

"Too windy," Powell responded. "You'll get hammered on the rocks before you've gone ten feet."

"Not if you get low enough. The canyon will act as a buffer."

Powell cut him a look. "You like to live dangerously, don't you, Campbell?"

He shrugged. "Is there any other way?"

Powell grinned and grabbed the joystick with both hands as he took the chopper down and tried to establish zero airspeed. After several minutes of bucking and pitching, the helicopter was finally situated over the mouth of the canyon.

Throwing off his headset, Aidan climbed into the back and fastened his harness. The JetRanger was specially fitted with an electric hoist that could be operated by the pilot, but until they knew the situation below, a quick insertion into the canyon was the safest bet.

Slipping his radio into his shoulder holster, Aidan opened the jump door to a blast of wind and rain. Balancing himself in the doorway, he threw down a rope and, then snapping his figure eight onto the cable, fast-roped down into the canyon.

Rappelling was the easy part. The canyon walls shielded him from the wind, but the moment he spotted the woman lying on a ledge about fifty feet down, Aidan knew they were in trouble.

She didn't appear to be conscious, although he knew she had to be on some level in order to have sent the signal. She lay beneath a narrow outcrop of rock that wouldn't have offered much in the way of protection from the storm. Her clothing was in tatters, her face covered in mud, and her hand, where she gripped the flashlight, was raw and bleeding. She must have tried to grab on to anything she could find to halt her momentum as she fell.

Aidan glanced up, his attention scaling the canyon wall. How she'd managed to survive a fall from that distance was a mystery. And a real testament to her will to survive.

Maneuvering over to the ledge, he unclipped from the rope and quickly knelt beside her. She opened her eyes when he touched her, and by the look of terror on her face, would have screamed if she'd had the energy. Instead, she tried to huddle even deeper into the overhang.

"It's all right," Aidan said to her over the rain. "I'm here to help you."

When she didn't respond, he said gently, "I'm not going to hurt you. But I have to find out how badly you're injured before I can get you out of here. Can you move?"

After a moment, she nodded and, uncurling herself, scooted toward him.

"Good. Excellent." He eyed her carefully. "Can you stand?"

"I...don't know." Her voice was barely a whisper, and she sounded so frightened and hopeless that it made Aidan want to wrap his arms around her right then and there. She was small, only about five-four or so, and he doubted she weighed much more than a hundred pounds soaking wet. Her hair was matted with mud, but he thought she was a blonde. Her eyes were dark blue and very intense.

He had the impression that she was an attractive woman, but he could see very little of her features through the mud and grime. Not that it mattered. Getting her out of the canyon and to a hospital was his only concern at the moment.

She tried to stand but couldn't quite manage it even when he helped her. Her knees collapsed and he eased her back onto the ledge.

"Okay, no problem. We'll do this another way."

He turned and said into the radio, "Powell? I've got the woman, but she's in pretty bad shape. I'm going to get her into a harness, and then you'll have to hoist us out."

"Copy that. Make it quick, Campbell. If we get caught in a down draft, we're all dead meat."

As quickly as he could, Aidan slipped leg rings over the woman's thighs and tightened the harness belt around her waist. Grabbing the cable, he used another figure eight to fasten her harness to his, then he radioed Powell.

"All set! Take us up!" To the woman, he said, "Put your arms around my neck. Don't worry. I've done this before," he assured her when they lifted off the ground and she gasped.

The first moment of dangling in midair was always the worst. "Don't look down," he advised.

To answer, she tightened her arms around his neck.

He could feel her muscles tense even beneath her layers of clothing. She was very light in his arms, but he had a feeling she was a lot stronger that she looked. She would have to be, to survive what she'd been through.

They were about thirty feet from the mouth of the canyon when a gust of wind buffeted the chopper, knocking it forward. The hoist cable shrieked and went taut as it lashed against the JetRanger's hull.

The woman screamed. The hoist moaned. And Aidan swore.

"It's okay!" he yelled above the roar of the blades. "I've got you! Just hold on tight!"

Overhead, Powell forced down the helicopter's nose to stabilize the aircraft, but the maneuver caused the cable to swing away from the hull, and all of a sudden, Aidan saw the wall of the canyon rushing to meet them.

He tried to twist around so that he would take the brunt of the collision. His left shoulder smashed into the rock, and as pain shot down his arm, he momentarily released his hold on the woman and they were jerked apart by the impact.

To Aidan's horror, he heard the figure eight snap, and the woman screamed again as she began to slip free. For a moment, her arms clutched at him wildly, and then Aidan grabbed her. As their eyes met, he recognized the terror in her eyes. He'd seen it before, in another woman's eyes, a split second before she slipped from his fingers and fell to her death.

He blinked, willing away the memory as he clung to the woman's arm. Elena had struggled blindly in her terror. She'd twisted and flailed and begged him not to let her fall.

"I don't want to die. Please, Aidan..."

That same plea was in this woman's eyes, but amazingly, she didn't panic, which would have made Aidan's job that much more difficult. When he shouted for her to grab his other hand, she had the presence of mind to do exactly that.

"Just hold on, okay?"

She nodded, her focus never leaving his.

They dangled over the canyon for what seemed an eternity, but she never once lost her cool. She had to be in pain, not just from the fall, but from the way he clutched her arm. She didn't so much as flinch.

When they were finally hoisted up to the chopper, Aidan hauled her onto the ski and. then boosted her through the jump door. Only then did he breathe a sigh of relief.

He climbed in behind her, slid the door closed and turned. She'd collapsed on the floor and gone into convulsions. Throwing off the harness, he knelt beside her.

"Get us out of here!" he shouted up to Powell.

"I'd love to do just that," Powell shouted back. "Unfortunately, we've got a little problem."

They were trapped in a wind shear that kept dragging the helicopter downward. As the tail slewed about, it came dangerously close to the wall.

"Come on," Aidan said under his breath. "Come on!"

Powell practically yanked the joystick out of the floor to give them lift power. For a moment, he was forced to ride the wind backward, getting closer and closer to the wall until he could maneuver the chopper around and fly with a tailwind out of the canyon.

While Powell battled the wind, Aidan cut off the woman's wet clothing. Beneath all those soggy layers, her skin was like ice. He rubbed her arms and legs, trying to create enough friction to warm her up.

Rousing, she clung to him for a moment, as if she didn't yet realize that she was safe.

"You'll be okay," he assured her. "We just have to get you warmed up."

"Don't let me go," she whispered.

"I won't. I promise."

She was tiny, but surprisingly curvy, and her muscles were rock hard. At the moment, though, Aidan was more interested in the temperature of her body than in its shape.

"F-freezing," she gasped.

When he had her clothes off, he wrapped her in a blanket, then pulled her into his arms and held her close to his own warm body. She still couldn't stop shaking.

"Is she going to be okay?" Powell shouted.

She'd better be, Aidan thought grimly as he held her tight. He couldn't afford to lose another one.

Chapter Three

Thursday, 0900 hours

Kaitlyn came awake with a start. She'd been dreaming that she was falling, and she gasped as she tried to sit up. A firm hand on her shoulder pressed her back down.

"Try to take it easy."

That voice! Kaitlyn knew it.

She couldn't place it, but she knew it…

The dream was still so fresh in her mind that she almost expected to feel wind rush past her face as she fell, but instead, she was lying perfectly still in a nice, warm bed.

A hospital bed, to be exact.

Someone had brought her to Ponderosa Memorial, but she only had a vague recollection of being rushed into the E.R. Of bright lights burning into her eyes. Of urgent yet somehow soothing voices speaking to her and above her. She'd been examined and x-rayed…all of which had passed in a blur of pain and confusion.

She was still a little out of it, but not as disoriented as she'd been then. Maybe it was the pain that had snapped her out of the haze. She suddenly felt as if every bone in her body had been crushed. But she knew that wasn't the case. She was going to be fine. Someone had told her that.

She glanced up at the man whose hand was still her on her shoulder. He had dark eyes and an even darker expression.

"I know you," she blurted.

Something flickered in those dark eyes. "I hope so. We went to high school together. I'd be very disappointed if you didn't remember me."

Frowning, she continued to stare up at him until the lightbulb went on. "Phillip? Phillip Becker?"

His lips tilted slightly, but Kaitlyn had a feeling that for him the gesture was significant. Although she hadn't seen him in years, the few faint memories she had of Phillip Becker were of a somber, overstudious young man who rarely cracked a smile.

"What are you doing here?" she asked in confusion.

"I'm a doctor. I've been on staff here at Memorial for a couple of weeks."

Why hadn't she known about that? Word usually traveled fast in such a small town.

"What time is it?" she asked.

"A little after nine."

She glanced at the window. "But...it's daylight."

"Nine in the morning," he clarified. "You've been here all night."

"I have?"

"You don't remember being awakened every two hours? The nurses said you were responsive."

She had a vague recollection, Kaitlyn realized. She frowned as she tried to think back.

Dr. Becker took a light from his lab-coat pocket and bent to check the dilation of her pupils. Next, he held his finger in front of her face and moved it slowly back and forth. "Try to follow my finger," he instructed. When Kaitlyn did as she was told, he nodded. "Very good."

Very good. Evidently, she'd passed some kind of test. Yea for her. "How did I get here? I mean, I know how I got here. Someone brought me in, right? But I don't know…I can't seem to remember all the details."

"Two men brought you down the mountain in a chopper," he said absently as he glanced at her chart.

"A chopper?"

"A helicopter."

Kaitlyn wasn't confused by the term. She knew what he meant. But the word had conjured up an image that left her even more confused. A deep voice commanding her to hold on tight. Blue eyes staring deeply into hers as he ran his hands over her body. *"We just have to get you warmed up."*

Who was he? she wondered. *Where* was he?

"I can't seem to remember a lot of things," she realized on a note of panic. "What's wrong with me?"

"Nothing that a little rest won't take care

of," Dr. Becker assured her. "You have a mild concussion. That explains the disorientation and the memory loss. Short-term amnesia is fairly common with head injuries."

"*What?* I have a head injury?" Even more alarmed, Kaitlyn lifted her hand to her head and winced when she felt a bump the size of a goose egg near her right temple.

"Try not to worry. Your MRI and CT look fine. Other than a little soreness, you should be as good as new in a couple of days."

Relieved, Kaitlyn stared up at the ceiling. "Will I get my memory back?"

"It's hard to say. I've seen car-crash victims who could remember every single detail leading up to the trauma, including the song that was playing on the radio before impact. But they have no recall of the accident itself. Not even weeks, months, sometimes years later. I wouldn't worry about it," he said with a shrug. "There are worse things than forgetting a fifty-foot fall into a canyon."

She'd fallen fifty feet. Into a canyon. *God.*

Still exhausted, Kaitlyn closed her eyes. "I suppose you're right." It was strange, though, having a gap in one's recall. She had a feeling those missing moments would nag at her forever.

"Try to concentrate on the positive," Dr. Becker suggested. "You were trapped on that ledge for nearly twenty-four hours. Any number of things could have happened. I'd say under the circumstances, you're a very lucky woman. You had a lot of people worried about you." He nodded toward the door. "One of them is outside right now. She's already caused quite a stir in the waiting room this morning."

Kaitlyn looked up in surprise. "She?"

"Eden McClain." His eyes seemed to darken. "Normally, I'd suggest you try and get a little more rest before you start having visitors, but I have a feeling no one will get any peace around here until she sees for herself that you're okay."

That sounded like Eden. The wonder was that she hadn't been able to finesse or bulldoze her way in before now.

"Shall I let her come in for a few minutes?"

"Yes, of course." Although how Eden had

even known that Kaitlyn was missing, much less hospitalized, was another mystery.

Dr. Becker made a note on her chart. "Don't let her stay too long. As I said, the best thing I can prescribe for your recovery is plenty of rest."

"Can I have something for the pain?" Kaitlyn asked meekly.

Becker frowned. "Try to ride it out a little while longer. I'd like to monitor your reflexes for a few more hours, but if the pain doesn't ease up, I'll have the nurse give you something mild." He closed the chart and tucked it under his arm. "Good to see you again, Kaitlyn. Sorry it had to be under these circumstances."

"You, too…Dr. Becker."

"Phillip, please," he said briskly. "After all, we do have something of a past, don't we?"

He turned then and disappeared through the door, leaving Kaitlyn to wonder just what in the world he'd meant by his parting statement. A past? The two of them?

She didn't have time to ponder the question for long, however, because a second later, the door burst open and Eden McClain took center stage.

THEY'D KNOWN each other since they were fourteen years old, but Eden's intensity never failed to impress—and exhaust—Kaitlyn. She was always so focused and so supremely self-confident that Kaitlyn sometimes wondered if her friend had ever experienced even a moment of inadequacy. Somehow Kaitlyn doubted it.

The daughter of a logger and a dressmaker, she'd certainly come a long way since her humble beginnings in Ponderosa. Everyone in the state knew that Eden McClain was the driving force behind Governor Gilbert's reelection campaign, and Kaitlyn wouldn't have been at all surprised to learn that her friend harbored political ambitions of her own.

If so, she would be a force to be reckoned with. Feminine and gorgeous on the outside with her power suits and pearls, and hard as nails on the inside.

God help anyone who got in her way, Kaitlyn thought.

Eden walked over to the bed and gave her a quick hug. She always wore the same perfume, something dark and sensuous. She called it her "signature" fragrance, and she guarded the formula as jealously as a lost man might horde water in the desert.

"So how are you feeling?" Ending the embrace quickly, Eden straightened. She'd never been the demonstrative type, and the easy way in which Kaitlyn and her mother had expressed their affection had always made Eden uncomfortable.

"Like I fell off a cliff," Kaitlyn told her. "But never mind about me. What are you doing in Ponderosa? Shouldn't you be in Helena wowing Prince Petrov?"

Eden smiled. "Nikolai will just have to wait."

Kaitlyn's brows shot skyward. "*Nikolai?* Well, get you."

"Yeah, well, the informality is just for your benefit. In public, believe me, it's His Royal Highness all the way. At any rate, the moment I heard you were missing, I got here as quickly as I could." Eden gave her a reproachful look. "You had us all scared half to death, especially after the floodwaters receded and the state police found your vehicle. Your father was ready to call in the Marines."

Kaitlyn gasped. "Dad? He's not here, is he? Please tell me he's not in Ponderosa." In her own way, she loved her powerful father very much, but he could be trying under the best of circumstances. She wasn't proud of the fact that at thirty, she still found him somewhat intimidating, but at least she was honest enough to admit it these days.

"Lucky for you, he's still halfway around the world," Eden said. "I talked to your mother, too, just in case the news of your disappearance made it all the way to Texas. She was upset, naturally, but I managed to convince her that you're in perfectly capable hands here. She's staying put for the time being because evidently your grandmother has taken a turn for the worse."

"I know. Poor Nana." Kaitlyn lay back against the pillows and sighed. "Thanks for handling all that for me. I owe you one."

"You can repay me by telling me what possessed you to wander off so far," Eden scolded. "You were miles from the road when they found you. What on earth were you thinking?"

"I was trying to get a cell-phone signal," Kaitlyn explained. "And if that didn't work, I was hoping to make it to Eagle Falls before nightfall. I knew no one would miss me until the next day, and I didn't want to spend the night camped out on the side of road. It may sound crazy now, but I thought it was a good idea at the time."

"Yes, well, that seems to be your motto," Eden said dryly. "You've always been impulsive."

Kaitlyn couldn't deny the charge so she merely shrugged. "Anyway, I started walking and after that, everything…gets a little hazy."

Eden frowned. "What do you mean, hazy?"

"It seems I have short-term amnesia."

"Wow." Eden let out a long breath. "So… you don't even remember how you ended up on that ledge?"

Kaitlyn shook her head. "Not really, although I'd say it's pretty apparent that I fell.

Phillip says the amnesia may or may not be permanent."

"Speaking of Phillip..." Eden glanced at the door, then leaned toward Kaitlyn as she lowered her voice. "I just can't seem to wrap my head around the fact that he's a doctor. God only knows what his bedside manner is like. He always gave me the creeps back in high school."

"I think he's just shy," Kaitlyn said.

Eden gave her a look. "That's a kind way of putting it. Do you remember what a crush Jenny used to have on him? She was always such a needy little thing. But I suppose you can't blame her. An alcoholic mother, an abusive father...she was a walking cliché. She used to latch on to anyone who had a kind word for her."

"You know, I'd forgotten all about that," Kaitlyn said in surprise. "She did have a thing for Phillip, didn't she?"

"Big time. But good ol' Phil only had eyes for you. Like every other guy in town."

Kaitlyn could have sworn she heard a tinge of resentment in Eden's voice, but when she looked up, her friend's dark eyes were completely guileless. As was her smile. "Not your fault you were so darn irresistible. Besides, men are such suckers for blue-eyed blondes."

Kaitlyn gave her an exasperated look. "You're exaggerating, as usual. Besides, I don't recall you ever having a shortage of admirers. And from what I hear, you pretty much have Peter Gilbert wrapped around your little finger."

"Just goes to show, you can't believe everything you hear." Eden laughed, but there was a flash of bitterness in her eyes. "Forget about Peter. Tell me about that hunk of eye candy that brought you to the hospital yesterday. Aidan Campbell."

"Aidan who?"

Eden looked flabbergasted. "Don't tell me you've forgotten *him*. Because if you have, I'd say you need to have your head *re*-examined."

She hadn't forgotten him exactly, Kaitlyn realized, as that same image came back to her. The whirring blades, the strong arms, those eyes staring down at her.

"I think he has blue eyes."

"Blue eyes?" Eden gave a little laugh. "That's like saying Montana has a lot of trees. Yeah, he has blue eyes. Crystal clear and surrounded by lovely, dark lashes...I could go on, but I won't. Let's just say the man has the most gorgeous eyes I've ever seen and leave it at that."

"Wait a minute." Kaitlyn turned to glare at her. "How do you know what he looks like?"

"Because I met him last night. He came by the hospital to see how you were doing. You were resting so we didn't want to disturb you, but we had a nice little chat before he left."

"You were here last night? How in the world did you find out so quickly?" Kaitlyn asked in astonishment.

Eden merely shrugged. "You forget, my dear, I now have contacts all over the state. That and the fact that when I called the paper yesterday afternoon looking for you, the receptionist told me that you were missing. I came as soon as I could."

"You really didn't have to do that. I know how busy you are these days."

Eden waved a dismissive hand. "You'd do

the same for me." She pulled up a chair and sat down. "Now, where were we? Oh, yes. Gorgeous, blue eyes."

Kaitlyn was amused by her friend's rather obvious segue back to the subject of her rescuer. She'd never heard Eden sound quite so effusive. "So tell me about the rest of this guy."

"Oh, the rest of him isn't too shabby, either, if you like wide shoulders and sun-bronzed skin. A Mr. December if ever I saw one," Eden said, referring to the pinup calendar she and Jenny and Kaitlyn had drooled over one year in high school. Mr. December had been by far the hottest month and remained, to this day, the standard by which Eden judged all men. At least in her more shallow moments.

"A Mr. December?" Kaitlyn laughed. "I think you're exaggerating again."

"Oh, really? Why don't you judge for yourself then? He's in the waiting room even as we speak."

Kaitlyn glanced up at her in alarm. *"He's been here all night? Why?"*

"No, relax. He came in right after I did this

morning. He said he wanted to check in and make sure you're okay." Eden paused. "Do you want me to go get him?"

Kaitlyn ran her fingers through her hair. "I don't know. I must look like—"

"A hag? Yes, you're positively hideous," Eden agreed dryly. "But as luck would have it, I've brought you a care package." She placed a bag from Ferguson's drugstore on Kaitlyn's bed. "Hairbrush, lipstick, mascara. And if you're good, I'll go by your apartment and pack a few things for you before I leave today."

"You wouldn't mind? Hospital gowns can get a little drafty if you know what I mean." Kaitlyn rummaged through the bag. "You're a real lifesaver, Eden."

"Yes, that's me," she said airily as she headed for the door. "But a word to the wise…" She paused and glanced over her shoulder. Mischief glinted in her eyes. "You may have seen Aidan Campbell first, but I've already picked out a name for our firstborn."

EDEN REALLY HADN'T exaggerated, Kaitlyn realized when her rescuer walked into the room.

Aidan Campbell was about as dreamy as

a man could get, but his rugged features kept him from being *too* dreamy.

But, boy, oh boy, did he bring the shivers.

Wide shoulders…sun-kissed hair…bronzed skin. Eden had described him to a T, and his eyes—gorgeous indeed—had the unique ability to appear warm and cold at the same time.

He had the look of a man who could turn a woman inside out, and Kaitlyn's stomach fluttered with awareness as their gazes met.

A dozen images flitted through her head. His blue eyes staring intently into hers. His deep voice commanding her not to panic. His callused hands moving skillfully over her bare skin to warm her up.

And then she thought, quite inanely, *Why, this man has seen me naked. We haven't even really met yet and already he knows what I look like without my clothes on.*

She couldn't look at him without thinking about it.

"Kaitlyn?"

The sound of her name on his lips sent another shiver up her spine and a sophomoric blush to her cheeks. Kaitlyn wasn't the type to be swept off her feet by a good-looking man, but for the life of her, she couldn't seem to remember her own name.

An apologetic frown flickered across his brow. "I'm sorry. I've obviously come at a bad time. I can stop by later—"

"No! I mean, uh, that's fine. This isn't a bad time. It's a perfectly fine time. I'm… fine…" And obviously babbling. She stopped and drew a breath. "You must be Mr. Campbell," she said in a more poised tone.

"Aidan." He let the door close behind him as he crossed the room to her bed.

Up close, he seemed even taller than she'd first thought. Toned and athletic, he walked with the kind of easy grace that came with confidence and accomplishment. A man who knew how to get what he wanted and almost always did.

Kaitlyn suppressed a shudder as he extended a hand and took hers.

He smiled.

She smiled.

And fireworks exploded all around them.

Oh, wait…that was just inside her head, she realized.

She drew back her hand. "I'm not sure

what to say to the man who saved my life. A mere thank-you seems a bit lame."

He shrugged. "It'll do just fine, but I don't think I saved your life. You strike me as pretty resourceful. Not many people could have survived a tumble like that, much less the kind of exposure to the elements you had to face. I have a feeling if we hadn't come along when we did, you would have clawed your way off that ledge."

"You think so?" Kaitlyn was foolishly flattered by his praise. "But then…I might have broken a nail or something, so it's just as well you saved me the trouble."

He said quite seriously, "Have you checked your nails lately?"

She glanced down at her hands and winced. "You weren't kidding about the clawing, were you?" She hid them under the cover.

He grinned. "In any case, I'm glad you're okay."

We just have to get you warmed up.

Why couldn't she stop thinking about that? Especially now, when she felt quite toasty. And that smile! Where had this man been all her life?

How was it that their paths had never crossed in a place as small as Ponderosa?

His expression sobered. "You are okay, aren't you?"

"I will be." She adjusted the blanket. "No serious injuries, I'm happy to report. The doctor says I'll probably be getting out of here in a day or two."

"That's good news." He glanced around. "Mind if I sit?"

"Please." Kaitlyn motioned to the chair Eden had vacated. Now that she'd managed to regain her equilibrium, she was in no hurry for Aidan Campbell to leave. No hurry at all.

He pulled up the chair and sat down at her bedside. "Are you up to answering a few questions?"

"You sound like a cop," she said in surprise.

He shrugged. "I'm just curious as to what you were doing out in the middle of nowhere alone in a rainstorm."

"That seems to be the question of the day," Kaitlyn muttered. "I'm a reporter for the *Ponderosa Monitor.* I was on my way to Warden Green's press conference…" She trailed off. "You've heard about the prison break, I assume?"

"It's been all over the news for the past two days."

She nodded. "Anyway, I was on my way to the press conference when I got caught in the flood. I had to leave my vehicle and head for high ground. I was hoping if I kept walking, I'd be able to get a cell-phone signal. And I knew if I headed north, I'd eventually reach Eagle Falls."

He scratched the back of his neck. "And then you what?…walked off the edge into that ravine?"

"Well, see, that's where things get a little screwy," she admitted. "I can't seem to remember what happened. I must have stumbled in the dark. Or maybe I got caught in a mudslide." She lifted her shoulders helplessly. "I don't remember what happened. I only have a vague recollection of the rescue. I heard the helicopter and then I saw you staring down at me…the next thing I know, I'm in the hospital." She paused. "If you hadn't come along when you did, there's no telling how long I might have been on that ledge. I don't know who sent you and your friend out to look for me, but I'm grateful to everyone involved."

"Actually, we were already out there searching when we got the call that a woman was missing. But if you hadn't had the presence of mind to use your flashlight to send up a signal, we'd never have spotted you."

"It was the only thing I had in my pocket," Kaitlyn said. "I must have lost my cell phone when I fell. Anyway, when I heard the helicopter, I started clicking the light on and off and praying that whoever was up there would see it."

"And we did."

"And you did." She eyed him for a moment. "But now I have a question. You said you were already out there searching when you heard about me. Who were you looking for?"

"We were looking for the fugitives."

Kaitlyn frowned. "But…you said you're not a cop." Her tone sounded vaguely accusing.

"I'm not."

"A fed, then?"

"I'm a bounty hunter."

"A *bounty* hunter?" Kaitlyn would never have guessed that. Bounty hunters were oily little men who crept around in dark, sleazy places, weren't they? Aidan Campbell didn't fit that image at all. She bit her lip. "Wait a minute. You must work for Cameron Murphy."

It was Aidan's turn to seem surprised. "You know Murphy?"

"Only by reputation," Kaitlyn admitted. "His apprehension of Boone Fowler is practically legendary around here. I've been trying to get an interview with him for years. I'd give anything to know what his reaction is to the prison break. Maybe you could put in a good word for me."

She regretted the request the moment the words were out of her mouth, especially when she saw the shutters drop over Aidan's blue eyes. His expression, friendly before, became remote and chilly, and he stood abruptly. "I should get out of here and let you rest."

"No, don't go," Kaitlyn said in a rush. "I'm...sorry. That was extremely rude, considering you just saved my life. I don't know what came over me."

"You're a reporter after a story," he said coolly. "I understand that. But if you want my advice, you're wasting your time with Colonel Murphy."

"Why?"

"Because he has no use for reporters." Aidan headed for the door.

"Wait!"

He turned, his eyes wary, almost hostile. Kaitlyn's blood tingled at that look, and the thought occurred to her that Aidan Campbell was not a man she wanted as an enemy.

"What about you?" she asked hesitantly.

"What about me?"

"How do you feel about reporters?"

He gave her a look she couldn't quite define. "Most of the time they're a nuisance. Kind of like prickly heat or jungle rot. Not dangerous, just a real pain in the ass to have to deal with."

Chapter Four

Jacob Powell waited for Aidan at the small airfield on the edge of town where he'd set the chopper down earlier. While Aidan headed off to the hospital, Powell had stayed behind to tinker with the JetRanger's engine. He was giving the tailboom a visual check as Aidan walked up.

"So how's the patient?" Powell asked.

"Not too bad, considering. She has a mild concussion, some cuts and bruises, but nothing serious. The doctor says she'll be fine in a day or two."

Powell jotted something in the logbook he'd been holding, then closed the cover and tossed the binder into the cockpit. "Well, that's good news. Were you able to talk to her?"

"Only for a few minutes. She wasn't able

to tell me much. Evidently, she's suffering from short-term amnesia and doesn't remember anything before or after the fall."

"That seems a little convenient."

Aidan frowned. "What do you mean?"

"We're assuming she fell off the ravine in the dark. Or maybe got caught in a mudslide. What if it didn't go down that way?"

"What's your point?" Aidan asked more sharply than he meant to.

Powell slipped on his sunglasses. "Murphy knows someone out at the prison. He was able to get a copy of the visitor's log, and Kaitlyn Wilson's name kept coming up. For the past month or so, she's made weekly trips out to the Fortress, and she always signs in to see Fowler."

Aidan tried to hide his shock. "You're sure about this?"

"Positive. I don't know about you, but the timing of those weekly visits has me a little concerned."

"You don't actually think she's in cahoots with Fowler, do you? Come on, she's a reporter for the local paper. The five-year anniversary of the bombing is coming up. Makes sense that she'd try to talk to Fowler."

"On five separate occasions? And answer me this, Campbell. What the hell was she doing up on that mountain in the middle of a storm? That's rugged terrain under the best of conditions."

Aidan shrugged. "She says she was on her way to the prison to cover the warden's press conference when she got caught in the flash flood."

"Yeah, but we found her miles from the road," Powell reminded him. "What made her wander so far off the beaten track? And now she has amnesia? I don't know. Something about her story doesn't smell right to me."

"Careful," Aidan warned. "Your suspicious mind is working overtime."

"Damn right I'm suspicious. You and I both know that Fowler and his men had help breaking out of the Fortress, and now someone's obviously aiding and abetting them on the outside. Think about it. They've got to be getting supplies from somewhere. Did it ever occur to you that the woman in question could have had an ulterior motive for being up on that mountain?"

The accusation annoyed Aidan, but for the life of him, he couldn't figure out why. "What the hell kind of supplies could she deliver on foot in a downpour?"

"The information kind." Powell climbed into the chopper and waited until Aidan was buckled in beside him. "Look, I know it's a long shot, but I'm just saying I don't think we should necessarily take her at face value, that's all."

"Okay, I'm down with that," Aidan said grudgingly. "But what is it you're suggesting we do?"

"Keep an eye on her, for starters. See if she makes any more wilderness excursions. And maybe we ought to go back and take a look around the area where we found her. Any objections?"

"Why would I object?"

"You seem to have formed an attachment to this woman. I guess you've got that victim-savior thing going on."

Aidan gave him an irritated look. "Do you even know what you're talking about?"

"Come on, Campbell. Admit it. It's a pattern with you. You always fall in love with the women you rescue. Or is it that they fall in love with you and you just don't know how to say no?"

"You're full of it, you know that?"

"So I've been told." Powell adjusted his headset, then started the engine. Over the *whop-whop* of the blades, he yelled into the mouthpiece, "So how'd she clean up?"

Aidan pretended not to hear him as he fiddled with his own headset. "What?"

"The woman. How does she look with all that mud cleaned off her face?"

"She looks…fine." *Damn fine.*

Powell grinned, but he said nothing else.

TWENTY MINUTES LATER they were on the pad at Big Sky Bounty Hunters headquarters, a remote outpost in the middle of the Montana wilderness. Built in the log-cabin style, the rustic building housed one of the most efficient and high-tech companies of its kind in the country.

Outfitted with the latest GPS tracking-and-surveillance equipment, the bounty hunters

employed by Cameron Murphy could effect-
ively pursue fugitives anywhere in the world.
And with the JetRanger III, a fleet of four-
wheel-drive vehicles, ATVs and snowmo-
biles, the rugged terrain they often found
themselves in posed few problems.

In the five years since Cameron Murphy
had resigned his commission in the service
and founded the company, Big Sky had become a phenomenal success. Recruiting
heavily from the ranks of the men he'd once
commanded provided him with the kind of
loyalty and skilled operatives no ordinary
firm could hope to match. And his distin-
guished military service had allowed him to
maintain close links with law-enforcement
bodies nationwide, including the FBI, which
often gave his organization another leg up on
the competition.

Aidan was the latest recruit, having left
the service a year ago following a SAR mission gone bad. The former commandoes
who'd preceded him to Montana—Jacob
Powell, Trevor Blackhaw, Bryce Martin, and
the others—had welcomed him back into the
fold, but none of them, with the exception of

Murphy, knew the details of Aidan's resignation. He intended to keep it that way.

Some of the men were sitting around the conference table in the war room when he walked in, and while they waited for Powell to finish his postflight check on the Jet-Ranger, Aidan briefed them on the rescue operation the day before.

When he finished, Murphy got up to pour himself some coffee. By this time, Powell had joined them, and he grabbed a cup of coffee, too, before taking his place at the conference table.

"You don't seriously think this woman is helping the fugitives," Murphy said doubtfully as he came back over to the table.

Powell took a sip of his coffee. "She may not be guilty of anything except bad judgment, but let's at least play devil's advocate here. I've got a gut feeling there's more to her story than she's telling—whether she remembers it or not. You saw the visitor's log. We know for a fact that she went out to the prison to talk to Fowler on at least five separate occasions. That alone is suspicious."

"We don't know yet whether he actually

agreed to see her or not," Murphy pointed out. "I'm still working on that."

"Even if she did, she's not the first reporter to trek out to the Fortress to see Fowler," Aidan said.

Powell shot him a look. "Yeah, but combine it with this latest business, and something stinks to high heaven. If she got caught in the flood, why not get to safety and just wait it out? Why take off up the mountain, alone, unarmed, in bad weather with night coming? Wouldn't she assume that someone would come looking for her?"

"She said she was trying to get a cell-phone signal," Aidan reminded him. "And barring that, she hoped to make it to Eagle Falls before nightfall."

"I can buy that," Riley Watson drawled from the end of the table. In his more unguarded moments, like now, Watson was prone to letting his Texas roots show, but he could just as easily disguise his accent when he wanted or needed to. "There's a long stretch on Route 9 between Ponderosa and the prison that's a dead zone. Could be that's where she ran into trouble."

Powell shrugged. "Okay. But walking ten, fifteen minutes in either direction to try and get a signal…that's one thing. When we found her, she was miles from the road and nowhere near Eagle Falls. And now she conveniently says she doesn't remember what happened."

Murphy's dark gaze moved to Aidan. "What do you think, Campbell?"

In all honestly, Aidan didn't quite know what to think. He would have sworn Kaitlyn was telling the truth when he'd first walked into her hospital room earlier, but she'd tipped her hand with her comment about interviewing Murphy.

And now to find out that she'd been out to the prison to see Fowler…

Aidan had crossed paths with ambitious reporters before, and he knew only too well how far some of the more ruthless ones were willing to go to get a story. It wasn't inconceivable—although unlikely—that a journalist with more guts than common sense could have tried to make a deal with Fowler.

"I think an involvement with Fowler is pretty remote," he said slowly. "I'm inclined to believe her story, but I guess it wouldn't hurt to check her out."

Murphy nodded. "We can run a background check on her, but I don't think it'll turn up anything. For what it's worth, I know the woman slightly. Her father is something of an icon in media circles. He's won every award the industry has to offer and then some. He interviewed me once, and I found him to be fair, for the most part. However, he's also something of an arrogant, self-important tool. I imagine he'd be a pretty hard act to follow."

Aidan folded his arms as he leaned against the window frame. "What do you mean?"

"A daughter who thinks she has something to prove might do something stupid if she thought she could get a major story out of it. Since you've already got an in with her, Campbell, I'd like you to do the follow-up. Let's not tip our hand to her yet. Just go talk to her again and see if what she has to say sets off any alarm bells."

"Do you want me to put her under surveillance?" Aidan asked.

Murphy considered the question for a moment. "I'll leave that up to you. I agree her involvement is pretty unlikely, but at this point, we can't afford to overlook any possibility. We know Fowler's getting help from somewhere. Which brings me to Craig Green's press conference."

Setting aside his coffee, Murphy got up from the table. "Most of you have already been briefed, but for those of you who were still out in the field when Clark and I got back from the prison, I want to bring you up to speed on the main points Green covered."

As he began to pace, he counted off the points on one hand. "One…at approximately 2200 hours on Monday night, a commotion breaks out on Cell Block C where inmates serving life sentences are housed. Fowler and his cohorts begin hurling racial and anti-American slurs at some of the other prisoners. A fight breaks out and quickly escalates into a brawl. Then a full-fledged riot ensues.

"Two…the facility goes into a complete lockdown. Fowler and his gang are subdued and led off to solitary confinement while the guards try to restore order to the cell block.

"Three…a guard goes to check on Fowler

and the others the following morning and finds their cells empty. Somehow the prisoners managed to escape during the riot, but no one knows how or who helped them. And no one's talking, either. Not the inmates or the guards."

"It had to be an inside job," Michael Clark ventured. Experienced in strategic intelligence collection, the man's ability to read body language and speech patterns bordered on the uncanny. "I normally operate under the theory that you can learn more from a subject by what he doesn't say than from his actual words. In Craig Green's case, though, his statement was pretty damn revealing. He announced that he'll be leaving his post within the next six months, and I find his timing curious, to say the least."

"Did he give a reason?" someone asked.

"Age, poor health, pressures of the job, wanting to spend more time with his family…" Clark trailed off with a shrug.

"Sounds like the usual BS a man shovels to the public when he's being forced out," Bryce Martin observed quietly. Introverted and brooding, the man rarely spoke during these meetings, but when he did, the other bounty hunters were inclined to listen.

"That's the way it sounds to me, too, but my sources indicate otherwise," Murphy said. "Frankly, I'm surprised the man wasn't fired a long time ago. He's been dogged by rumors of corruption for years, and I wouldn't be surprised if he has a nice, fat off-shore bank account somewhere. My guess is he'll wait until the dust settles around the prison break, and then he'll flee the country before the feds can pin anything on him." He cleared his throat. "Which is why I want to take a closer look at him. Like Clark said, the prison break was obviously an inside job, and Green's the strongest suspect we have so far. But at the same time, we'll have to be careful not to step on any toes."

"Yeah, the feds do have a tendency to get a little territorial, don't they?" Trevor Black-haw said with a grin. Despite his tame demeanor, this half Cherokee former commando was legendary in Big Sky Country for his fierce interrogation tactics known to break even the most iron-willed men.

"I've spoken to my FBI contact and informed him of our intensions," Murphy said. "So far, the Bureau hasn't thrown up any barriers, but he did let something slip. And gentlemen…" He placed his hands flat on the table and leaned forward, his eyes gleaming. "This is where things get interesting."

Aidan's blood quickened at the look on Murphy's face. It was obvious something was up. Something big.

"It seems an army of special agents swarmed into Montana *before* the prison break."

"They must have gotten wind of it somehow," Watson speculated. "Someone talked."

"It's possible." Murphy straightened from the table and continued to pace. "But I'm inclined to think the deluge of federal agents into the state has something to do with Nikolai Petrov's visit."

That made sense to Aidan. Petrov's whirlwind tour of the country had been all over the news for weeks. Ever since his speech before the United Nations General Assembly, he had been elevated to near godlike status by an adoring press and legions of enamored fans. But Petrov was more than just a pretty face. Openly defying his father before the world in order to call attention to the plight of his people had taken guts.

Aidan had spent some time in Lukinburg, and he knew just how oppressive and ruthless the current regime had become in recent years. Once a satellite of the USSR, the tiny country had gained its independence during the 1990s, and the government had reverted back to the monarchy that existed prior to Soviet domination.

On his ascension to the throne, King Aleksandr had been heralded by his people as a heroic freedom fighter who had never lost touch with his people. But a tricky road lay ahead for the ruler and his fledgling nation. After the collapse of the Soviet Union, Lukinburg found itself in desperate financial straits, and under Aleksandr's leadership, tight governmental regulations were instituted to allow the stagnant economy to rebound.

But in spite of the country's burgeoning prosperity, Aleksandr sought more and more control over the private sector until he became, in the end, what he had always despised…a greedy, arrogant despot with seemingly little compassion for his own people.

The already dangerous situation in Lukinburg had worsened in recent months when rumors began to filter out that Aleksandr had used chemical weapons against a rebel faction and that he was now quietly in the market for purified uranium.

Once those rumors were confirmed at the now-famous United Nations showdown between father and son, the world body could no longer ignore the oppression of the Lukinburg people. Sensing a weakening in the Security Council's former rigid stance against military intervention, Nikolai had used his instant celebrity to take his case directly to the public.

And if current polls were any indication, his PR blitz was a resounding success. A fact that hadn't gone unnoticed by Aleksandr, who had recently declared his son an enemy of the state.

All this went through Aidan's head in the blink of an eye as he considered everything that Murphy had told them.

He glanced at his former commander. "An

assassination attempt," he said. "That could be why the feds are pouring into the state."

Murphy nodded. "Exactly my thought. An attempt on Nikolai Petrov's life on American soil could set off an international incident with catastrophic consequences. Which means Boone Fowler won't exactly be at the top of the feds' priority list. That's where we come in."

There was something in Murphy's eyes… a look that Aidan hadn't seen since their last clandestine mission together. It made his own adrenaline spike as he watched Murphy's face settle into a grim mask of resolve and anticipation.

"A substantial bounty has been placed on each of the fugitives, but I'll be honest with you, men. It's not about the money for me. This one is personal. I intend to bring Boone Fowler in *by any means necessary.* If any of you have a problem with that, now's the time to speak up."

No one said a word. They all knew of the bitter history between Murphy and Fowler. The brutal militia leader had killed Murphy's sister in the government building bombing five years earlier, and very nearly murdered the woman Murphy had eventually married. In return, he'd hunted Fowler and his followers down and sent them to prison for life.

Fowler had sworn revenge on Murphy and his family at the trial, and now he was out. If he could find a way to get to Murphy's wife and daughter, he'd do it in a heartbeat.

Which meant the bounty hunters would have to get him first, *by any means necessary.*

If Kaitlyn Wilson was somehow involved, God help her.

"All right, that's all," Murphy said, drawing the meeting to an end. "You each have your assignments. Good hunting and Godspeed."

As the men filed out of the room, Murphy called Aidan aside. He walked over to the table where the colonel still stood.

"Is there anything else I should know about your rescue mission yesterday?"

"What do you mean?" Aidan asked warily.

"You left out a few of the details when you briefed us earlier. I talked to Powell last night while you were still at the hospital. Sounds like things got a little dicey out there."

Aidan shrugged. "There was an equipment malfunction, but nothing we couldn't handle."

"That's what Powell said, but I'm glad to hear it from you."

Aidan knew what the colonel was getting at, but he wasn't buying it. "It doesn't change anything," he said flatly.

"Doesn't it?" One brow rose slightly. "I'd say it changes everything. No matter how hard you tried to kill yourself before I found you six months ago, yesterday proves you've still got what it takes."

Aidan's voice hardened. "And no matter how many people I drag out of a canyon, Elena Sanchez is still going to be dead."

Elena would continue to be the one who haunted Aidan's sleep every night. The one who woke him up in the darkest hours with her screams and her terrified pleas.

"Don't let go of me! Please, Aidan! I don't want to die!"

She'd been so young and so beautiful. An

innocent pawn caught up in the ravages of war but somehow managing to cling to that elusive dream of a better life for her and her family.

And she'd loved Aidan as no woman had ever loved him before, or ever would again.

Chapter Five

"She's alive."

Rage exploded like a mushroom cloud in Boone Fowler's chest, but he kept his head bent to his work. He knew how to control his emotions. Nine months of solitary confinement had taught him that.

Somewhere deep in the abandoned mineshaft, he could hear the steady drip-drip of water, and the sound, for the past half hour or so, had become a torturous monotony. He would have to tune it out, he supposed. So many things to tune out…

"Did you hear what I said?" his visitor demanded indignantly. He shoved a lantern aside and placed his hands flat on the table. "That reporter…Kaitlyn Wilson. She's still alive."

Fowler looked up then. The cavern was full of shadows, and for a moment, he thought he saw one of them move. But it was only his imagination. Or a draft causing the flame inside one of the lanterns to shift. He had sentries posted at the mine entrance. No one who didn't belong could get in without his knowing.

"That's impossible," he finally said. "It's a hundred-foot drop to the floor of that canyon. There's no way she could have survived a fall like that."

"Well, apparently she did. And somehow she managed to sustain only minor injuries. Two of Cameron Murphy's men found her yesterday afternoon huddled on a ledge halfway down the canyon."

At the mention of his nemesis's name, Fowler's hand curled around the pearl-handled knife he'd been sharpening. But when he spoke, his voice remained measured and calm. "You should have let me take that bastard out the minute I got out of stir."

"And risked everything we've worked so hard for? I don't think so." His companion straightened and began to walk around the cavern. His looming shadow followed him to and fro. "We didn't go to the trouble and expense of breaking you out of the Fortress just so you could pursue your own petty vendetta."

Fowler wasn't used to being spoken to in such a disrespectful manner, and he didn't like it one bit. There wasn't much he could do about it now, though. The time for settling old scores would come soon enough, and until then, he would bide his time. If there was anything he'd learned in prison, it was patience.

He bent to his work again. "What about the woman? Has she talked?"

"Not yet. It seems she's suffering from short-term amnesia. She doesn't remember anything prior to her fall, but her condition could change at any moment. We can't let that happen."

"Don't worry about it." Fowler laid aside the whetstone and carefully tested the blade with his thumb. Satisfied that the edge was razor sharp, he closed the knife and slipped it into his pocket.

"You'll take care of her?" At Fowler's nod,

the man placed a briefcase on the wooden crate they'd been using for a table and snapped open the lid to reveal stacks of hundred-dollar bills. "Your first installment, along with instructions for the next job." He handed Fowler a large envelope. "You'll get the rest when the mission is completed."

Fowler opened the envelope and, after extracting the contents, rifled through the information that included aerial photographs of railroad bridges, maps of the area and copies of itineraries.

"You've been as thorough as usual," Fowler remarked. "Some of this stuff didn't come cheap."

"That's not for you to worry about. You should know by now that money is no object. But there is one thing that does concern you. The next job needs to look like an accident."

"An accident?" Fowler slid the documents and photos back into the envelope and glanced up. "You don't think the authorities will get a little suspicious after what we did to the other guy?"

"What we *did* was necessary to garner some of the information contained in that envelope. Besides, with any luck, his body won't be found for days, maybe even weeks."

"Yeah, but the feds are going to be out looking for him. That'll make our job a lot riskier," Fowler warned. "A man like that can't just disappear without all hell breaking loose."

"I told you before, we've planned for every contingency. Herr Schroeder was a player. He liked fast cars and beautiful women, and he frequently traveled without bodyguards to accommodate his married mistresses. The word has gone out in certain circles that he's off with his current paramour, the wife of a very prominent diplomat. He won't be missed for at least another week."

"That all sounds well and good, but I still say the feds won't believe an accident."

"And I say you need to stop buying trouble," his companion snapped. "If there's no evidence of a terrorist attack, then the National Transportation and Safety Board will conduct the preliminary investigation. The FBI's hands will be tied, and by the time they untangle themselves from all the red tape, it'll be too late. The only thing that can derail us now is the woman."

Fowler glanced up with a smile. "You need to stop buying trouble," he taunted. "Because that bitch is as good as dead."

SOMEONE WAS TRYING to kill her!

Kaitlyn let out a scream, but the sound was muffled by the pillow pressed tightly against her face. She couldn't breathe! Dear God, she was going to die!

With every ounce of her strength, she fought off her attacker. The intensity of her defense must have caught him by surprise, because she heard him grunt as he lost his grip on the pillow and she knocked it away.

For one split second, Kaitlyn found herself staring up into the face of her would-be killer. He wore a ski mask to hide his features, but she could see his eyes. Dark and gleaming, they were staring back at her.

She recognized those eyes...she had looked into them before.

And then he stuffed the pillow over her face and pressed with what seemed like superhuman strength. Kaitlyn still fought him, but the battle was useless. She could feel consciousness slowly slipping away from her....

KAITLYN WAS STILL GASPING for breath when the nurse came running into her room. "Did you see him?" she panted.

"See who?"

"He was here just a second ago." Kaitlyn searched the room as her hand flew to her throat.

The nurse hurried over to her bed and pushed her gently back against the pillows. "Just take it easy, honey. You had a bad dream, but you're fine now."

Kaitlyn's heart was still pounding as she looked up at the nurse in confusion. "Bad dream?"

"I'll say. I heard you scream all the way down at the nurse's station."

Kaitlyn grabbed the woman's arm. "Someone was in my room! He tried to kill me!"

"Tried to kill you? Oh, goodness me, that must have been one doozy of a nightmare," she said with a chuckle.

"It wasn't a nightmare!" Kaitlyn cried frantically. "Someone came in here and tried to smother me with a pillow! I think…I think it was Boone Fowler."

"Boone Fowler! Oh, honey, that awful man is long gone from around here. You just had a bad dream, that's all."

Kaitlyn brushed off the woman's hand. "Please, you have to believe me. We need to call someone…the police…"

The nurse gave her a sympathetic smile. "No one was in here, sweetie. Not Boone Fowler or anyone else. I've been at my station for hours. I would have seen someone come in and out of your room. The whole floor has been as quiet as can be all night."

"But…he was here. I saw him."

The nurse tucked in the sheet and smoothed out the wrinkles.

"I know you don't believe me, but he was here," Kaitlyn insisted. "I know what I saw, and I think we should call the police."

"Let's not go dragging the police over here at this hour, okay? I'd just have to tell them the same thing I've been trying to tell you. No one has been in or out of your room all night. Except for Dr. Becker, of course."

Kaitlyn's eyes sharpened. "Dr. Becker was in here?"

"He was called back to the hospital for an emergency, and came by a little while ago to look in on you. He does that a lot. He's a very good doctor. You're lucky to have him."

Kaitlyn wasn't sure why, but she found the idea of Phillip Becker coming into her room while she slept more than a little unsettling.

"I think he's still in the building," the nurse said. "Why don't I page him? Might make you feel better to talk to him."

"It would make me feel better if you'd call the cops," Kaitlyn muttered.

"Just talk to Dr. Becker first, okay? It won't take me a second to find him. Try and stay calm until I get back."

Stay calm? Boone Fowler had come into her room and tried to kill her. How was she supposed to stay calm about that? Kaitlyn wondered.

But...what if it had been a dream?

Now that she thought about it, why would Fowler, or anyone else, want to kill her? She might have rubbed a few people the wrong way in her career as a reporter, but she couldn't imagine anyone wanting to harm her.

But it had seemed so real.

Her door opened, and Dr. Becker strode in, followed by the now-anxious-looking nurse.

"Hello, Kaitlyn. Hattie tells me you've had a restless night."

That was putting it mildly, but Kaitlyn didn't quibble with his choice of words. She was beginning to feel a bit foolish. What if it really had been nothing more than a bad dream?

Dr. Becker came over to her bedside and looked down at her. His appearance was so different that Kaitlyn might not have recognized him if she hadn't known he was coming to her room. He was in street clothes for one thing—dark slacks, a black leather jacket—and his five-o'clock shadow made him look a bit sinister. Which was not at all the way Kaitlyn remembered Phillip Becker. Studious, yes. Introverted, yes. Maybe even creepy, as Eden had said. But…sinister?

When he picked up her wrist, she found herself wanting to recoil from his touch, but she didn't know why.

"Your pulse is a bit elevated," he murmured. He measured it again, then glanced up from his watch. "Now what's this about a nightmare?"

Before she could speak, the nurse interceded. "She insists that Boone Fowler came into her room and tried to smother her with a pillow."

Blurted out like that, it did sound ridiculous, Kaitlyn thought bitterly.

Dr. Becker's brows shot skyward. "Boone Fowler? Isn't he one of the fugitives we've been hearing so much about lately?"

The nurse nodded. "She was watching the news when I came in here earlier. She probably saw Fowler's picture or something. God knows, it's enough to give anyone the willies, knowing those escaped convicts are out there somewhere."

Kaitlyn glared up at them. "I wish you'd stop talking about me like I'm not even here, and, yes, I did watch the news earlier, and, yes, Boone Fowler's picture was all over the broadcast. But I don't think what I experienced was a nightmare. It was too real."

"I'm not sure it was a nightmare, either," Dr. Becker said slowly.

Kaitlyn's mouth dropped in shock. "You mean…you believe me?"

"That someone came in here and tried to kill you? No. But I believe that you believe it."

Kaitlyn frowned. "What's that supposed to mean?"

"I think you had a hallucination. You didn't dream your assailant. You actually saw him here in the room with you."

"A hallucination?" Kaitlyn said doubtfully. "How is that different from a dream?"

"You were awake. That's why it seemed so real to you."

"I don't understand," she said weakly.

"There are numerous medical and psychiatric causes of hallucinations, but in your case I believe it to be the result of PTSD—post-traumatic stress disorder."

"From my fall, you mean."

"Any fearful trauma can produce symptoms. Think of it as the aftershock of an extremely threatening event. In its acute phase, PTSD occurs directly after the trauma and is not only treatable but curable. The chronic phase can come along much later and is only treatable, but…I'm getting way ahead of myself here. It's much too early to think in those terms. We'll cross that bridge when and if we need to."

PTSD.

Kaitlyn lay back against the pillows. She didn't know whether to be relieved or alarmed.

"The pain medication I prescribed for you earlier is quite mild, but it's possible the hallucination was caused in part by a reaction to the drug. I'll change your dosage—"

"No! No more drugs." From here on out, Kaitlyn wanted to keep a clear head.

Dr. Becker hesitated. "Very well. But if the pain becomes too severe, I want you to call the nurse. I'll have her check in on you hourly, and then I'll come by in the morning when I make my rounds. In the meantime, get some rest. You're still recuperating."

"I'll try." But Kaitlyn wasn't making any promises. Hallucination, bad dream, whatever the hell she'd experienced earlier, she wouldn't wish it on her worst enemy.

She lay back against the pillows, but it was a very long time before she closed her eyes.

Chapter Six

Friday, 0900 hours

By the time Aidan got to the hospital the next morning, Kaitlyn was out of bed, fully dressed, and—except for a few bruises on her face and some scratches on the backs of her hands—looked amazingly fit for someone who had been through what she had.

He hardly recognized her, in fact. Dressed in pinstripe navy trousers and a white sweater, she appeared cool, calm and collected, nothing at all like the bedraggled woman he'd found curled in the fetal position on a ledge two days ago.

Her hair had been tangled and matted with mud when he'd first seen her, but now it hung in a sleek sheet down her back, gleaming so pale in the morning sunlight that it almost appeared to glow.

Aidan had known all along that she was an attractive woman. But he'd had no idea she was drop-dead gorgeous.

He couldn't get over how tiny she was and how fragile her features seemed. But he'd witnessed firsthand just how tough she truly was, both mentally and physically. She'd fallen—or slid—fifty feet into that canyon and she'd gone fighting, scratching, and clawing every inch of the way. Except for mostly superficial wounds—bruises, scratches and some torn fingernails—she'd come through the ordeal virtually unscathed.

And later, when the clip had snapped on the hoist cable and she'd nearly fallen to her death yet *again,* she still hadn't panicked. Now that took guts.

Aidan had another memory of her, too, but he'd been trying his damnedest to banish that image. He didn't want to keep picturing what she looked like without her clothes on. It didn't seem right. She'd been at her most vulnerable at that moment, and Aidan wanted to remain dispassionate and objective about the whole thing, like a doctor with his patient.

But who was he kidding? He was no doctor. He was just a man, and Kaitlyn Wilson was one hell of a woman.

She'd been naked in his arms, for God's sake, and vulnerable or not, there was no way in hell Aidan could forget that.

Don't let go of me, she'd implored him as he held her. *I won't,* he'd answered, and Aidan suddenly wished that that was a promise he'd been able to keep. Because right now, he would have liked nothing more than to have his arms around her again.

It didn't make sense, this attachment he had to her. Maybe Powell was right. Maybe he did fall in love with all the women he rescued. First Elena...and now Kaitlyn.

He watched her until she turned and saw him at the door.

"Oh...hello," she said in surprise. "I wasn't expecting to see you this morning." She seemed unsure of herself, as if unnerved by his sudden appearance. Served her right. She'd caught him off guard, too, just by standing there in the morning sunlight. "To tell you the truth…I was a little worried I'd never see you again."

She would have probably been better off if he hadn't come back, but here he was. He had a job to do, and he might as well get to it. "I came to apologize." He stepped into the room and let the door close behind him.

"Apologize? What for?"

"I overreacted when you asked me to put in a good word for you with Murphy. I apologize for insulting you and maligning your profession. It's no excuse, but we've had some bad experiences with the press in the past. In our line of work, it's best to keep a low profile."

"I understand. No hard feelings." When she smiled, her eyes crinkled at the corners and her lips curled enticingly. Aidan couldn't help noticing that she had a great mouth.

It took a little willpower, but he tore his attention from her lips. "I just came to say that if you want to pursue an interview with Murphy, that's between the two of you. I won't intervene on your behalf, but I won't try to stop you, either."

"That's fair." She extended her hand. "Shake?"

"Sure, why not?" Aidan walked over to take her hand, noting that in spite of her small stature, she had a firm grip. He liked that about her, too.

In fact, he couldn't think of much he didn't like about Kaitlyn Wilson, other than her profession. And the possibility that, if Powell's hunch proved correct, she might be hiding something.

"Maybe we should just pretend yesterday never happened," she said. "Although I've remembered some things that might make that a little difficult."

"You've got your memory back? That's great." He searched her face for a telltale twitch or flicker.

She didn't seem to notice as she absently fingered the black duffel bag she'd been packing when he first walked into the room. "I still don't remember falling. That part is a complete blank. But I've been having some flashbacks about the rescue. Bits and pieces have been coming back to me all morning. Something happened to the rope, didn't it? It broke or something."

Aidan nodded. "The figure-eight clip that

fastened our two harnesses together snapped. I've never seen one do that before, even under tremendous stress."

"I started to fall and then you grabbed my hand and held on to me. Which means you saved my life twice yesterday." Kaitlyn's hand trembled slightly as she fumbled with the zipper on the duffel, and Aidan noticed now the dark circles under her eyes, which he hadn't been able to see from the doorway.

"I did what I'm trained to do," he said with a shrug. "You're the real hero here. If you hadn't kept your head, we could have been in real trouble."

"Kept my head?" She gave a strange little laugh. "I was scared out of my gourd!"

"It's called grace under pressure. You didn't panic or struggle. You kept your cool and that made all the difference."

She drew a deep breath and released it. "I think you're giving me way too much credit, but whatever. I'm just glad everything turned out the way it did. And now I can't wait to get out of here and put the whole thing behind me."

Aidan glanced at the duffel. "You're

going home today? That seems a little fast, doesn't it?"

"Dr. Becker wanted to keep me another day, but I badgered him into releasing me. I couldn't face spending another night in here. Not after…" She trailed off as something dark flickered in her eyes. She turned away with a shudder.

"Not after what?" Aidan said sharply. "Did something happen?" He could almost hear Powell riding him for getting so protective.

Aidan tuned him out as Kaitlyn glanced up at him.

She opened her mouth to say something, then shrugged and looked away. "Oatmeal that tastes like cardboard and scrambled eggs the consistency of rubber. That's what happened."

"Yeah, I'm not a big fan of hospital food, either. But I have a feeling that's not what you were about to say."

"No, you're right. Something happened last night. Not a big deal really, just kind of strange." She paused. "I had a hallucination. Never had one of those before," she tried to say lightly, but Aidan could tell that she was still shaken by the experience.

"What kind of hallucination?"

"Oh, it was a good one. Boone Fowler came into my room and tried to smother me with a pillow."

At the mention of Fowler's name, Aidan's gut tightened. "What makes you think it was a hallucination?"

Her brows lifted. "Maybe because, with an army of law-enforcement agents on his tail, I seriously doubt he'd show up in my hospital room in the middle of the night. Especially considering, I've never even met the man."

She hadn't seen him? What about her visits to the prison? Aidan wanted to ask her, but he remembered Murphy's warning not to tip his hand yet. "Maybe it was a dream," Aidan said slowly, his gaze searching her face.

"No, it was too real to be a dream. Actually, according to the doctor, hallucinations aren't all that uncommon following a trauma. And I guess Boone Fowler makes a strange kind of sense since I was on my way to cover Warden Green's press conference when I got stranded. Plus, Fowler's picture is all over the news." She lifted her hands. "Case closed."

Was it? Aidan wondered.

"Anyway, besides homicidal hallucinations, I really do feel so much better this morning. It's amazing what a shower and clean clothes can do for your morale." She was trying to laugh the whole thing off, but Aidan wasn't amused. He had a bad feeling that something more was going on here, whether Kaitlyn knew it or not.

Before he could say anything, though, a nurse rolled in a wheelchair. "Dr. Becker signed your release papers," she said cheerfully. "You're all set."

"That's great, but I didn't expect it to be quite so soon." Kaitlyn checked around the room, as if to make sure she hadn't forgotten anything. "I should call someone to come pick me up."

"I can give you a lift," Aidan offered.

"Oh, I couldn't ask you to do that. Not after everything you've already done for me."

"You're not asking, and it's no trouble. I'm already here. Besides—" he turned to the nurse "—looks like you're ready to kick her out of here."

The nurse grinned. "We won't put her out on the street or anything, but we've always got a shortage of beds, so if you're going, the sooner the better."

"Well, in that case…" Kaitlyn gave him a tentative smile. "If you really don't mind…"

"I don't. Where should I pick her up?" he asked the nurse.

"Pull your car around to the E.R. entrance. I'll bring her out that way."

"Here, why don't I take this?" He reached for the duffel. "I'll meet you outside in a few minutes."

"Okay. And…Aidan?"

He turned at the door and glanced back.

"Thanks again. For everything."

She looked so sincere and sounded so earnest that Aidan almost felt guilty for what he was about to do.

THE DUFFEL CONTAINED nothing but a pair of silk pajamas, a robe and an assortment of toiletries—the usual fare one would need for a short stay in the hospital.

Aidan hadn't expected to find anything incriminating—certainly nothing that would link her directly to Boone Fowler or the Montana Militia for a Free America. But as much as he liked and admired Kaitlyn, he couldn't discount Powell's intuition about her, because the man's instincts were usually dead-on. Powell wasn't prone to making snap judgments or wild leaps. If he thought there was more to Kaitlyn's story than met the eye, chances were he was right. Aidan just wondered if Kaitlyn even knew what that something was.

Zipping the duffel, he stowed it in the back, then started his Jeep. He pulled up to the E.R. entrance just as the nurse wheeled Kaitlyn through the glass doors. He got out and hurried around to help her inside.

She groaned as she climbed into the front seat.

"God, I feel like I'm a hundred years old," she said after he slid in behind the wheel.

"You're bound to be a little stiff for a few days," he said sympathetically.

"A little stiff? Every muscle in my body aches. I haven't hurt like this since I let my friend Eden talk me into a yoga class." She let her head drop back against the seat, as if the effort of climbing into the Jeep had left her exhausted.

"Are you sure you're okay?" Aidan asked worriedly.

She didn't open her eyes. "I will be. Just give me a minute." She drew in another breath and seemed to steel herself against the pain. "Okay, I'm ready."

He waited for a moment, but when she made no move to fasten her seat belt, he reached over to snap the harness into place. "Here, let me help you…"

She opened her eyes then, and for one split second, Aidan found himself staring back at her. He couldn't glance away. He didn't want to. Something stirred deep inside him, an attraction he'd been fighting since he'd walked into her hospital room that morning.

No, he'd felt it before that even. Yesterday. And the day before, when she'd been clinging to his hand for dear life.

She was a beautiful woman, no question. Even more beautiful than Elena, and he would never have thought that possible. But the two women couldn't have been less alike.

Elena had been tall, thin, frail. Dark, sultry eyes and gleaming black hair.

Kaitlyn was a blue-eyed blonde, and so petite that Aidan could easily lift her in one arm. But there was nothing frail about her. Not even now, when she was so obviously in pain.

Her face was only inches from his, and he found himself staring at her mouth. She had the most gorgeous lips he'd ever seen. Soft, full, lush. He wanted to trace those lips with his tongue. Kiss her so hard and so deep that neither of them would be able to think straight for a week.

He was turned-on just thinking about her body pressed against his, and it shamed him to remember that she'd just gotten out of the hospital. The woman had very nearly lost her life.

It didn't seem to matter. Aidan couldn't stop thinking about her, and he couldn't look away to save his own life.

Her breath quickened as if she'd suddenly become aware of his attraction. She remained perfectly still, her eyes locked with his, the aphrodisiac scent of her shampoo making him want to bury his head in her hair.

He had the strangest feeling that if he kissed her right now, she just might let him.

Before she could change her mind, he closed the distance, brushing his lips against hers, and when she didn't resist, he deepened the pressure.

Her mouth opened like magic beneath his. He slipped his tongue inside and she responded with a little jerk. But she still didn't pull away.

Instead, she kissed him back. So fiercely it took his breath away. Somehow he hadn't expected that, and he wondered fleetingly if he'd opened a Pandora's Box. How far was he ready to take this?

Apparently, quite a bit farther, and it didn't seem to matter that they were in full view of anyone exiting or entering the hospital. If she wanted them to start ripping off their clothes right then and there, he was game. All she had to do was say the word.

He slid his hand up her arm and tangled his fingers in her hair, drawing her even closer. She came willingly, cupping his face in her hands as she moved her mouth against his.

She was a great kisser, which also surprised him. She had the face of an angel, but the way she turned him on was anything but angelic.

Groaning softly against his mouth, she pulled away with a little gasp.

Aidan felt instantly remorseful. She was still bruised and battered, and he hadn't exactly been gentle. "Did I hurt you?"

"What?" She looked almost as dazed as when he'd found her on that ledge. "Hurt me? No, you didn't hurt me." She put a hand to her mouth. "What just happened?"

"I kissed you."

"I know, but why?"

"Does there have to be a reason?"

"I would hope so. You don't just go around kissing strange women, do you? Seems to me that would be a good way to get your face slapped."

"You didn't slap me," he reminded her.

"I know." She let out another breath. "I don't understand why."

She looked adorable, so dazed and perplexed. Aidan wanted to kiss her again but decided not to press his luck. He straightened and moved back over to his place behind the wheel. "It's not so hard to figure."

"No? Then why don't you clue me in?"

"You've just come through a terrifying ordeal. You were nearly killed. It's not unusual to have some sort of emotional release after an experience like that."

"Okay," she said thoughtfully. "That explains why I didn't slap you. It might even explain why I kissed you back. But I still don't understand why you kissed me in the first place."

"That's easy. You're hot."

Her eyes widened—in outrage or shock, Aidan wasn't quite sure which. He reached forward to start the ignition. When he turned back to her, she was still staring at him.

"That can't be the first time you've ever heard that," he said.

"I guess not. But…" She bit her lip. "You may have saved my life, but…you scare me a little."

Her candor took him by surprise. She had a habit of doing that…taking him by surprise. "That's funny," he muttered. "Because I was just thinking the same thing about you."

He put the Jeep in gear without waiting for her response and pulled away from the hospital. Once they were on the road, he glanced at her. She hadn't said a word since they'd left the parking lot. "You'll have to give me directions to your place."

"Sure, but would you mind dropping me off at the diner instead? I'm starving," she said sheepishly. "I guess it's doing without real food for so long. But you don't have to wait for me. I only live a few blocks from there. I can walk home."

She'd barely had the strength to climb into the Jeep, but Aidan didn't think it was a good idea to point that out to her. Instead, he said, "I seem to have worked up an appetite myself. You don't mind if I join you, do you?"

"Uh, no, not at all. I'll even pick up the tab," she said with a smile. "It's the least I can do."

DAMN, DAMN, damn, Kaitlyn thought worriedly. She couldn't get rid of the guy.

Not that kissing his brains out was exactly the way to go about it, but she desperately needed a breather. A little time to herself to think about everything that had happened over the past few days, but mostly to wonder how in the heck she'd ended up in the arms of a man she'd never even known existed until two days ago.

Maybe it had been nothing more than an emotional release, as he'd said. Kaitlyn had heard of people having comfort sex as a way of reaffirming life when someone close to them died. Maybe that was what she'd been doing with her tongue stuck down Aidan Campbell's throat. Reaffirming life.

No matter the reason, it just wasn't like her to get so caught up in the moment, and it scared her. She wasn't a virgin, and she certainly was no prude, but she didn't like losing control that way. She was impulsive in almost every other aspect of her life, but when it came to romance and sex, she rarely let down her guard. It made her too vulnerable, and she didn't particularly want to open herself up to hurt.

But all that aside, now was just not a good

time for her to be falling for a new man, even one who had saved her life. She'd finally made a decision about her future, and that was that. She didn't want to start second-guessing herself because of some guy.

Oh, for God's sakes. You'd think he asked you to have his baby or something.

He'd just kissed her, and it would never happen again.

It probably wouldn't happen again.

It might not happen again.

And even if it did happen again, what was the point in getting all worked up over a few innocent kisses?

It wasn't like she was planning on having sex with him, or anything.

Now that really would be stupid.

What she needed to do was concentrate on the things about him that she didn't like.

Hmm.

Okay, this was going to take some thought, but she'd come up with something. Mr. December over there couldn't be *that* perfect.

Kaitlyn had never met a man yet she couldn't pick apart, given time and opportunity.

The attraction probably wouldn't last through breakfast.

Another day at the most and Aidan Campbell would be nothing but a memory.

Chapter Seven

Okay, this was not working out at all the way she'd hoped, Kaitlyn grudgingly acknowledged. The moment Aidan had taken her arm to help her out of the Jeep, her knees had gone all weak and her heart had started to pound. It was getting to the point where she could hardly even look at him without blushing, which was just ridiculous.

Thankfully, the diner was in a lull between the breakfast and lunch crowds and they had their choice of tables. Kaitlyn decided on a booth near the front windows rather than one of the cozier corner tables. With all the natural light pouring in through the plate glass, she figured it would be an excellent opportunity to nitpick some imperfection in Aidan's seemingly perfect appearance.

And after a few minutes of conversation, if it went the way she anticipated, he'd probably start to annoy her the way most men seemed to these days.

She could handle this, no problem. Even if she couldn't get him out of her system as quickly as she'd hoped, so what? She was no stranger to physical attraction and, allowed to run its course, a relationship like this never amounted to anything more than a few weeks—months at the most—of casual dating and, all too often, unsatisfying sex. Her attraction to Aidan was an anomaly…like snow in July or something. It was never going to last.

Okay, enough with the obsessing!

With an effort, Kaitlyn turned her attention to the menu as a slender, pretty waitress brought over glasses of water.

As she bent to place them on the table, Kaitlyn said, "Hi, Patty."

"Hey, Kaitlyn. Heard about what happened to you out on Route 9. You okay?"

"I'm fine. Starving, though. I'll have my usual."

The waitress shook her head. "Where you put it all, I'll never know." She turned to Aidan and said quite seriously, "In case you're picking up the check, I'd better warn you about this girl. She eats like a horse."

What a lovely image Patty had just planted in Aidan Campbell's head. Perhaps it was just as well, Kaitlyn decided.

"Patty, this is Aidan Campbell. He and a colleague are the ones who rescued me. Patty and I went to high school together."

Aidan extended his hand and the two of them shook.

"You must be new in town," Patty commented. "I don't think I've seen you in here before." *And I'm sure I would have remembered, her expression implied.*

"I travel a lot."

"That so?"

Instead of commenting further, as her tone invited, Aidan glanced down at the menu. "I'll have a stack of pancakes and a side order of sausage."

"You want hash browns with that?"

He glanced at Kaitlyn, who shrugged. "Go for it. You won't catch me passing judgment. I'm having the Hungry Man Special."

"Bring me the hash browns," he said with a wink.

Patty got all flustered as she gathered up the menus, then giving Kaitlyn a knowing look, hurried off to the kitchen.

"So," Aidan said as he straightened his silverware, "you're a hometown girl."

"More or less. My family lived in Washington, D.C., until I was a teenager, but we always spent summers here. When my parents divorced, my mother and I moved out here full-time."

"That must have been quite a culture shock," he said. "This place is about as far removed from the Beltway as you can get."

Unrolling her own silverware, Kaitlyn placed her napkin on her lap. "Not really. I already had a lot of friends here, and I've always loved Montana. There's just something about it that keeps you—I don't know—grounded."

"Not a lot of opportunities for an ambitious reporter, I wouldn't think."

Kaitlyn tried not to stare at him as they talked. If he had a flaw, she had yet to find it. "Who said anything about being ambitious?"

"You told me you've been trying to get an interview with Cameron Murphy for years, and I know firsthand how blunt he can be. Plus, you braved some of the worst flooding this area has seen in years to get to Warden Green's press conference. I'd say that's pretty ambitious."

"Really? I call it doing my job." Kaitlyn took a sip of her water. "Besides, good reporting is good reporting, no matter where you are. Working for a small paper is not easy. People don't realize. We don't have all the modern technology that the big news organizations employ these days. We don't use stringers and we don't rely solely on the wire services for our leads. We do our own research and legwork, conduct our own interviews, and we maintain a distinction between the news section and the editorial pages. You can't always say that about some of the larger papers these days."

"Not only ambitious, but passionate," Aidan murmured.

The way he said *passionate* made her think

of that kiss again. Honestly, how old was she? Twelve? "Is there anything wrong with being passionate?" she demanded.

"Not at all. You seem to be pretty passionate about a lot of things."

Her gaze narrowed. Was that some kind of crack?

"I'm talking about food." He nodded toward the counter. "Looks like your friend is having some trouble fitting everything onto one tray."

Kaitlyn supposed she should have been embarrassed by the size of her order, but she'd always been a big eater and she hadn't had a decent meal in days. If Aidan was turned off by her appetite, then so be it. Who cared what he thought anyway? He was just a guy who'd saved her life. She didn't need to impress Aidan Campbell. Besides, if that kiss hadn't impressed him, nothing would. She'd kind of impressed herself even.

Kaitlyn took another sip of her water as Patty unloaded the tray: plates of pancakes dripping with real butter, hash browns fried to a golden crisp, fluffy scrambled eggs seasoned with green peppers and onions, sides of sausage and bacon, and, for good measure, homemade biscuits.

"Good God," Aidan muttered, his expression ranging from shock to admiration and finally settling on dismay. "Don't tell me you're going to eat all that."

"Shut up and pass the syrup," Kaitlyn said as she munched on a piece of bacon. It was the perfect amount of doneness—not too crisp, not too limp—and she sighed happily. "I've always had a fast metabolism so I figure I've got another five years before I have to start watching my weight. Until then I fully intend to enjoy my carbs."

He eyed her plate. "I think carbs are the least of your worries."

She shrugged. "Whatever. I like food. So sue me."

"You're passionate about food and you're passionate about your job. What else should I know about you?"

Oh, no, you don't, Kaitlyn thought. *You are not going to draw me out. We are not going to exchange intimacies. You are not going to make me like you.*

"You were right earlier when you said that

I'm ambitious. For a lot of reasons, I've been playing it safe. Pretending that I don't care about success and recognition. But lately I've been thinking that maybe it's time to go after what I want, because I don't want to look back ten or twenty years from now and have regrets." *What the hell?* Now *why* had she told him all that?

"Here's to bigger and better things then."

"To different challenges."

"I'll drink to that." He lifted his water glass and eyed her over the rim. "So how does your father figure into all this new ambition?"

Kaitlyn stared at him in surprise. "You know my father?"

"Only by reputation. Logan Wilson, right? The war correspondent." He paused. "Those are some mighty big shoes to fill."

His insinuation irritated the heck out of Kaitlyn and she thought almost in relief, *Oh, yeah, this guy's Mr. Perfect, all right.* Except for the insensitive bastard part. "For your information, I'm not trying to follow in my father's footsteps," she snapped. "Some of us like to make our own way in the world."

"Whoa, time out. I didn't mean to hit a nerve."

She lifted her chin. "You didn't." But, of course, he had hit a nerve.

"Look, I'm sorry." He set aside his fork and leaned toward her. "That was a stupid thing to say."

"It's okay." And oddly enough, it was.

Kaitlyn blinked, surprised that her anger—not to mention her pride—could be pacified so easily by such a wimpy apology. Where was the groveling she usually expected? Where was a little righteous indignation when a girl needed it the most?

Damn those eyes of his. They could melt a heart at twenty paces.

"That's okay," she managed to say primly. "It's just…"

"You don't owe me an explanation. You don't owe me anything. I really am sorry."

Yes, you are, would have been her response to any other man on the planet. With Aidan Campbell, she just wanted to kiss and make up. Over and over and over.

She was *so* in trouble here.

"Okay, you did touch a nerve," she admitted, rubbing the back of her neck. "My father has been on the ground in every war this country has been involved in for the past forty years. He won a Pulitzer for his reporting from Vietnam and another for a series he did during the Gulf War. He even interviewed Saddam Hussein a few months before the fall of Baghdad, and he's one of the few western journalists that King Aleksandr has allowed to stay in Lukinburg while he prepares the country for war. So, yeah, you're right. Those are some big shoes to fill."

Aidan said slowly, "Your father is in Lukinburg?"

She shrugged. "Kind of ironic, isn't it, considering that Aleksandr's son, the crown prince, is right here in Montana, of all places. I have a contact in the governor's office who's trying to set up an interview for me."

"Shouldn't be too hard," Aidan said dryly. "Nikolai Petrov loves publicity."

"He's a regular PR machine," Kaitlyn agreed. "But he doesn't do that many one-on-one interviews, and I'm not exactly Diane Sawyer or Katie Couric here. If I could pull off an exclusive at the same time my father is reporting from Lukinburg…" She trailed off, letting Aidan draw his own conclusion.

"It would be quite the family coup," he finished.

"Wouldn't it just?"

"You'd pretty much be able to write your own ticket anywhere you want to go."

"That thought has occurred to me," she admitted.

"So if the Petrov interview means that much to you, why weren't you in Helena covering his arrival instead of stranded in a flood on your way to the warden's press conference?"

"Because the prison break is a huge story, too, and because…" She glanced out the window.

"Go on."

"I have my reasons, okay? Let's just leave it at that."

He started to say something else, but Patty came to clear the table just then, and thankfully, the interruption provided Kaitlyn an excuse to change the subject. She didn't want to talk about her connection to Boone Fowler, or her intense need to see the man returned to prison where he belonged. She didn't want to explain why she'd betrayed her best friend or the part she'd played in Jenny's death. She didn't want to explain any of that to Aidan Campbell because, suddenly, she didn't want him to know the kind of person she'd once been. The man had risked his life to save hers. Call her crazy, but she didn't want him to think it had been a big waste of his time.

"My turn," she said, glancing back at him.

He lifted a brow. "Your turn?"

"To ask the questions." She blotted a water ring on the table with her napkin. "That's what we ambitious reporters do, you know. We ask questions. Lots and lots of questions."

He seemed a bit wary all of a sudden. "What is it you want to know?"

Where to begin? "Why did you decide to become a bounty hunter?"

"I needed a job and Murphy offered me one. Next question."

"Hold on, I have a follow-up."

"No follow-ups."

She gave him a wry look. "You've done

this before, I see. Okay, consider this a separate question then. Did the two of you serve together in the military?"

"He was my commanding officer before he resigned his commission five years ago."

"After his sister was killed in the bombing, right? He came back here to look for Boone Fowler."

"You'll have to ask him about his motives. I don't make it a habit of answering for someone else." He was definitely being cagey now, which wasn't fair considering she'd practically spilled her guts to him.

Kaitlyn had so much more she wanted to ask him, but she put the interrogation on hold as Patty came over again to bring the check. Kaitlyn reached for it, but Aidan beat her to it.

"You should let me get that," she protested. "I owe you."

"You can get it the next time." He grabbed his wallet and pulled out some bills.

Wait a minute, Kaitlyn thought. Was there going to be a next time?

Did she want a next time?

Now *that* was an excellent question.

LATE THAT AFTERNOON, Aidan and Powell returned to the canyon where they'd found Kaitlyn two days earlier. Michael Clark accompanied them, and after Powell established a hover, Aidan and Clark fast-roped down to the edge of the canyon to have a look around.

Aidan didn't really believe they'd find evidence of Kaitlyn's complicity with the fugitives. Even if she had gone up there to meet Boone Fowler—which he still seriously doubted—any footprints or ATV tracks that would have proved she hadn't been alone would have been washed away by the rain.

Aidan agreed with Powell on one thing, though. Fowler and his gang were getting help from someone. It had been more than four days since the escape, and in spite of roadblocks, aerial surveillance and an all-out manhunt by local, state and federal law-enforcement—not to mention Big Sky Bounty Hunters—the fugitives remained at large. Dozens of leads continued to pour in, but most of them had yet to pan out.

Given the tight net that had quickly

dropped over the area, Aidan doubted the fugitives had managed to make it across the state line. More than likely, they were holed up somewhere nearby, which led him back to the original question. Who the hell was helping them?

They had to have a hideout where someone brought supplies and information. Aidan figured the accomplice was someone local, someone familiar with the terrain, and if that someone turned out to be Kaitlyn, she would be in big trouble, no matter her reason. Even he wouldn't be able to save her in that case.

But the woman wasn't stupid. No matter how much she wanted to impress her father, she hadn't come across as desperate. Ambitious, yes, and judging by her actions, she could also be impulsive. But making a deal with Boone Fowler for a story would be akin to selling her soul to the devil.

Still…there had been that moment in their conversation when she had evaded his question about her decision to cover the prison-break story over Petrov. *"I have my reasons, okay? Let's just leave it at that."*

Finishing their exploration along the canyon rim, Aidan and Clark widened the perimeter of their search. The abandoned hunting lodge he'd pointed out from the air was about a hundred yards or so straight back into the woods. Making sure the surrounding area was secure, they approached the building with caution. Climbing the rickety steps, Aidan kicked open the door, and then, weapons drawn, they both went in.

On first glance, the place looked as if it hadn't been occupied in years. The large room reeked of mold and dust, and a layer of grime on the glass filtered the sunlight coming in through the windows.

The only furnishings in the room were a table and two wooden chairs, and the only outside door was the one they'd come through. Both Aidan and Clark made sure they didn't put their backs to it.

Moving stealthily about the room, Aidan took out his flashlight and probed the dim corners. Cobwebs hung from the beamed ceiling, but the stone floor was surprisingly clean.

He knelt and ran his hand over the surface. Nothing. Not even so much as a film of dust.

"What do you make of this?"

Clark came over and squatted beside him. He was dressed in fatigues the same as Aidan, and his dark hair was hidden by a cap pulled low over his features. "Someone's been busy."

"It's not just clean, it's been scrubbed," Aidan said. "Now, why would someone go to that kind of trouble?"

"Because they wanted to get rid of something, obviously." Clark took out his own flashlight. He bent low as he angled his beam across the floor. "Looks like they missed a spot." He got up and walked over to the table and chairs, then knelt again to run his light over the wooden legs. "Take a look at this."

Aidan crouched beside him to examine the dark splotches. Moistening the tip of his finger, he touched one of the spots, then brought it to his nose. "Blood," he said. "I'd say it's fairly fresh."

Clark's expression turned grim. "Maybe we'd better have a closer look outside. I'll take the back."

They exited the lodge, and while Clark headed around the building, Aidan stood at the bottom of the steps and tried to map the area in his head.

Route 9 lay south of the lodge. According to Kaitlyn's story, she'd followed an old hunting path northward up the mountain. Aidan knew the trail she meant, and assuming she'd more or less stayed on course, she would have ended up at the lodge. The ravine was a hundred yards to the west. For some reason, she'd veered off course and ended up on that ledge.

Locating the trail, Aidan stood at the edge of the woods and studied the area, trying to imagine what Kaitlyn might have seen when she came out of the trees. By then she'd probably been walking for at least a couple of hours through bad weather and difficult terrain. When she reached the lodge, she would have been cold, wet and exhausted. The logical thing to do would be to seek shelter inside from the storm.

Aidan traced what he imagined were her steps across the clearing, but instead of going inside, he walked over to the front window. He couldn't predict exactly how Kaitlyn would have reacted, but he'd seen her in action and knew that she wasn't prone to panic.

She might be impulsive at times, but she also knew how to keep her head. He'd stake his life that, rather than rushing headlong into the lodge, she would have checked things out first, especially if she had reason to believe someone else might be inside.

The window was several feet from the ground, but even someone as tiny as Kaitlyn would have been able to peer inside. The grime on the glass would have inhibited her view, but if a light had been on inside, she would have been able to see well enough.

Crouching beneath the window, Aidan searched the still-damp ground, not really expecting to find footprints, but what he did spot was even more interesting.

Digging the cell phone out of the mud, he cleaned it on his fatigues, then pressed the on button. Nothing happened. He wasn't surprised. The phone had obviously been there for a while. At least a few days.

He started to slip it into his jacket pocket, then paused as a conversation with Kaitlyn came back to him.

"If you hadn't had the presence of mind to

use your flashlight to signal us, we would never have spotted you."

"It was the only thing in my pocket. I must have lost my cell phone when I fell."

If this was Kaitlyn's cell phone, then it proved beyond a shadow of a doubt that she'd been at the lodge. She'd stood at that very window and perhaps witnessed something inside that had sent her fleeing blindly through the woods. Whether her fall had been accidental or the result of foul play was yet another question.

Clark said his name over the radio, and Aidan automatically turned his head to his shoulder to respond. "Go ahead."

"You'd better come see this."

"I'm on my way."

Pocketing the cell phone, Aidan straightened and hurried around to the back of the lodge. When he didn't see Clark, he called out his name.

"Over here!" the other man shouted.

Aidan followed his voice into the woods. About twenty yards in, he spotted Clark standing with his back to him, staring at the ground. When Clark heard him approach, he stepped back so that Aidan could see what he'd found.

The body had been buried in a shallow grave, but the heavy rains had left the head and upper torso partially exposed. He was a Caucasian male, but that was about the only thing Aidan could tell about him. Scavengers had already been at his face.

It was strange how suddenly quiet everything seemed. No birds in the trees. No rustle of leaves. There was nothing in the wind but the smell of death.

"This is the county boys' jurisdiction," Clark said after a moment. "We'd better notify the sheriff."

Aidan didn't respond. His mind was still on that cell phone in his pocket and the possibility that Kaitlyn had witnessed a murder. That she might even have somehow been a party to it.

He didn't really believe that, though. What he did believe was that she was in a world of trouble. If the killer hadn't known about her before, he would soon enough.

Once the investigation got under way, questions would be asked, leads would be followed, and Kaitlyn might as well paint a big bull's-eye on her forehead once the cops came knocking on her door.

Chapter Eight

Saturday, 0900 hours

Kaitlyn didn't rest at all well her first night at home. She'd so looked forward to being in her own apartment and sleeping in her own bed that she hadn't stopped to think how the silence of her own company might wear on her.

Even at night the hospital had been so full of sounds that—until her hallucination—Kaitlyn had pretty much been able to tune everything out. But at home, the individual sounds were what kept her awake—the rattle of pipes, the creaking of old floorboards, even the subtle hum of her refrigerator. Every time she closed her eyes, some new noise would startle her awake.

She must have gotten up a dozen times to

check her doors and windows, and once, when she'd glanced out at the street, she could have sworn she felt someone watching her from the dark.

She'd never been the nervous type, so she wondered if her new paranoia was another manifestation of post-traumatic stress. How else to explain this awful feeling that she was somehow in danger?

For goodness' sakes, who would want to hurt her? Other than Allen Cudlow, she had no enemies. None that she was aware of at least. And as for Allen, Kaitlyn had never been afraid of him, even when he was at his nastiest. He was sneaky and underhanded and even ruthless at times, but somehow she just couldn't picture him creeping through the darkness in his Dockers to do her in.

Could the paranoia be a side effect of the pain medication she'd been given at the hospital? Kaitlyn wondered. After she'd stopped taking it, she hadn't experienced any more hallucinations, but the residue in her system might be enough to cause a vague sense of unease.

There had to be some logical explanation for the personality change, because this sudden fearfulness, this awful sense of urgency made about as much sense as Boone Fowler coming into her hospital room in the middle of the night to smother her with a pillow.

Kaitlyn hated feeling so vulnerable. She'd never been afraid of being alone. In fact, she'd been living on her own for years now, and she'd always reveled in her independence. She knew her neighbors, but she wasn't overly cozy with any of them and that was the way she preferred it. Her garage apartment afforded her all the privacy she could want. She rarely even saw her landlady, Mrs. Morgan, except at the first of the month when she paid her rent.

Mrs. Morgan's house was at the end of a quiet street with only one neighbor to the right of her. Denny Vandermeer was a single man who liked to party, and his late-night antics could sometimes be a nuisance when Kaitlyn had to get up early for work the next day.

But on her first night home from the hospital, the laughter and music drifting up from his backyard became something of a comfort to Kaitlyn. Made her feel less alone. With so many people coming and going at all hours, she was perfectly safe, she kept reminding herself. And finally, just after dawn, she managed to drift off to sleep.

Sunlight streaming in through her bedroom window woke her up just after nine, and in spite of her exhaustion and the fact that it was a Saturday morning, Kaitlyn dragged herself out of bed, showered and dressed for work. The newspaper business knew no weekends, but Ken had encouraged her to take a few days off to fully recuperate. However, Kaitlyn had learned a long time ago that it was never a good idea to test her indispensability.

Both the prison break and Nikolai Petrov stories had the potential for huge national exposure, and if Kaitlyn could get her byline picked up by one of the wire services, it would be a tremendous leap forward in her career.

But it wouldn't be easy. Reporters from all the major news outlets were pouring into the area. Kaitlyn's only hope was to find a new angle, something no one else could bring to either story.

That was why an interview with Petrov was so important. As much as the prince seemed to enjoy the limelight, he rarely sat down with reporters. A one-on-one would catapult Kaitlyn to the big leagues. Aidan had been right about that. If she could get Petrov, then she'd be able to write her own ticket. But even with Eden in her corner, a Petrov exclusive was still a long shot.

And as for the prison break, she'd toyed with a number of ideas during her sleepless night, but only one held much appeal for her. She'd love to tell the story from a bounty hunter's perspective, but that would entail Aidan's cooperation, and despite his apology, he'd made his opinion of her profession crystal clear. Kaitlyn didn't think it too likely that he'd change his mind anytime soon.

Which was unfortunate. Because *that* would have been one hell of a story.

WHEN KAITLYN WALKED into the office a little while later, the receptionist, Sherry Jackson, jumped up from her desk with a loud squeal and hurried around to give Kaitlyn a big hug.

A tall, big-busted redhead, Sherry had the typical fair complexion and freckles that came with her hair color, but had somehow managed to escape the stereotypical fiery disposition. Kaitlyn had never known anyone as easygoing as Sherry. The woman was never in a bad mood and that was quite an accomplishment, considering how tempers often flared at deadline time.

Still beaming, Sherry held Kaitlyn at arm's length as she gave her a thorough once-over. "Well, honey, I have to say, you look pretty damn good for a woman who just knocked on death's door. But I hear you fell on your head, so that probably saved you."

Kaitlyn made a face. "Ha-ha, very funny."

Sherry's expression sobered. "You are okay, though, right? You know you scared us half to death, don't you, when you didn't show up for work on Wednesday morning. We knew something had to be wrong, so Ken and I called the county sheriff's office and told them you were missing."

"It's a good thing you did," Kaitlyn said, "or else I might still be out there on that ledge."

"You must have been so scared. I like to kid around with you and all, but I'm dead serious about this. Don't ever go off like that on your own again, okay? My heart couldn't take it. And besides, this place just wouldn't be the same without you."

Kaitlyn was touched by the woman's concern. "Oh, come on, you can't get rid of me that easily. You know what they say about a bad penny."

"Speaking of bad pennies..." Sherry cut her eyes toward the newsroom. "Cudlow has been in Ken's office all morning."

"What's going on?" Kaitlyn asked anxiously. "Anything I should know about?"

Sherry bit her lip. "Yeah, probably, but I don't think you're going to like it."

Kaitlyn had a sinking feeling in the pit of her stomach. "What is it?"

"Cudlow covered Craig Green's press conference on Monday. He drove up to the prison instead of going to Helena for Petrov's arrival."

Kaitlyn's mouth dropped in astonishment. "*What?* How did that happen?"

Sherry shrugged. "It seems there was a

decoy plane. Petrov landed sometime earlier in the day, and Cudlow managed to get wind of it. He decided there wasn't any point in driving all the way up to Helena just to camp out in front of Petrov's hotel, so he took the long way around to the prison and missed all the flooding."

"But why would he do that?" Kaitlyn asked in outrage. "He couldn't have known that I would get stranded. There's no way in hell he could have foreseen something like that."

"He said he heard about the road closings on the radio and anticipated that you might not be able to get through." Sherry gave Kaitlyn a sympathetic look. "I guess Ken was pretty impressed by his initiative because he's pulled Allen off Petrov and put him on the fugitive story."

"But that's *my* story," Kaitlyn said through clenched teeth. She could feel her blood starting to boil at the thought of Cudlow moving in on yet another one of her assignments.

It was like history repeating itself. Back when the previous editor in chief had been in charge, Cudlow had been given his choice of assignments while Kaitlyn had been reduced to nothing more than a glorified errand girl. She'd worked her butt off on story after story only to have Cudlow get the byline. She'd thought those days were behind her, but apparently not.

"We'll just see about that," she muttered as she spun toward the newsroom.

"Hold on, honey. I've got something else I want to tell you." Sherry glanced past Kaitlyn into the newsroom as if to make sure the coast was clear. Then she head-gestured for Kaitlyn to come back over to her desk.

"What is it?"

"I may know a way you can get back in Ken's good graces *and* stick it to Cudlow at the same time. You interested?"

"Is the Pope Catholic? Tell me more."

Sherry nodded, her eyes gleaming with excitement. "I've got wind of something that no one else here knows about yet. Not even Cudlow. You could probably blow him right out of the water with it."

Kaitlyn's enthusiasm waned. "Wait a minute. Your aunt hasn't had another premonition, has she?"

"No, but I'm telling you, you should go talk to her. Aunt Phyllis knows what she's talking about. She predicted the flood, you know. And five years ago, she knew something bad was going to happen before the federal building exploded. She could probably help the cops find Boone Fowler if they'd listen to her, but people around here are so narrow-minded—"

"Sherry. Get to the point."

"Okay." She motioned for Kaitlyn to come even closer, and when Kaitlyn was standing right beside her desk, Sherry said in a low voice, "How does murder grab you, honey?"

"Murder?"

"Shush." Sherry glanced back into the newsroom. "Keep your voice down. I'm not supposed to know anything about this."

"About what? Sherry, what are you talking about?"

"You remember my cousin, Abbey, right? The one who works at the hospital? She had to take some papers down to the morgue last night, and she said someone from the county coroner's office brought in a body while she was there. Everyone was acting all hush-hush about it, but she overheard just enough to know that the guy had been murdered. She said one of the younger deputies that accompanied the body looked pretty green around the gills, so she figured it must have been real gruesome."

"Do you know who the victim was?"

"They weren't able to make an ID, but an autopsy is scheduled for sometime this afternoon. You're still friends with Dr. Lake, right?"

Dr. Andrea Lake was a pathologist on staff at Ponderosa Memorial, but in addition to her duties at the hospital, she also served as an associate medical examiner for the state of Montana.

She and Kaitlyn went way back. Years ago, Andrea's family had lived next door to Kaitlyn and her mother, and although she was several years older than Kaitlyn, they'd always got on well. Both in their thirties now, they'd reached the age where a few years hardly mattered, and when Kaitlyn had moved back to Montana, she'd looked Andrea up and the two of them had become friends.

"Why don't you give her a call?" Sherry suggested. "Or better yet, go over to the hospital and talk to her."

Kaitlyn's gaze narrowed. "You're not trying to get rid of me, are you?"

"Oh, honey, don't be silly. We just got you back. But I think it might be a good idea if you cool down a little before you talk to Ken. And besides, this is a good lead, right?"

"Yeah, it is a good lead. Thanks, Sherry."

She perked up. "So you'll talk to her?"

"I'm on my way."

Because no matter what else was going on, murder was always big news in Ponderosa.

"THEY FOUND THE BODY, boss."

Boone Fowler glanced up from the maps he'd been studying and frowned. "The feds are getting sharper, it seems."

"The feds didn't have anything to do with it." Fowler's second in command hesitated, as if dreading to give him the rest of the information. "My contact says two of Cameron Murphy's men found him."

"Murphy." Fowler growled the name, personifying the sound with all the pent-up fury he'd been suppressing for the past five years. His rage terrified most people, but not Lyle Nelson. The two of them were like brothers. They'd been to hell and back together, and no one knew better than Nelson how deeply Fowler's hatred for Murphy ran, because he felt it, too. He wanted revenge just as badly as Fowler, and one day soon, they'd have it.

"I'll take care of him. Just say the word." Nelson's blue eyes gleamed at the prospect. He was proficient with guns and explosives, but like Fowler, he had a preference for knives. He could slice a man up in a thousand different ways and never break a sweat.

Suppressing his anger, Fowler clapped the man's shoulder. "Take it easy. It won't be long before Cameron Murphy and his men find out exactly what they're up against. But this time, we'll pick the time and place for the final battle, and they won't even know what hit them. Until then, we have a job to do. A new boss to pacify."

Nelson's eyes turned hard. "You know where my loyalty lies. To the Cause."

"As does mine. But to accomplish everything we've set out to do takes money, weapons, contacts. We need our new benefactor as much as he needs us."

"And you trust him?"

"I don't trust anyone. But if he isn't a man of his word, he'll live to regret it, just as Cameron Murphy will live to regret his interference. For now, though, we have a more pressing concern."

Nelson nodded. "You're talking about that reporter. She saw me kill him, didn't she?"

"She saw and heard too much, that's for damn sure, and if she puts it all together she could ruin everything." Fowler's grip tightened on Lyle's shoulder. "But don't you worry, my friend. We'll take care of Kaitlyn Wilson. All we need is a little help from one of our own."

CROSSING THE HOSPITAL lobby a little while later, Kaitlyn heard someone call out her name. Turning, she saw Phillip Becker striding toward her. She'd been heading for the elevators, but now she paused and waited for him to catch up to her.

"I thought that was you," he said, when he drew even with her.

Today he looked more like the guy she remembered from high school, Kaitlyn decided. No more leather jacket or five-o'clock shadow. He wore a lab coat over his street clothes and his dark-rimmed glasses, along with his rumpled hair, gave him a bit of an absentminded-professor look.

Phillip wasn't a bad-looking guy. He was tall and thin with dark hair and nice features. But with Phillip, there was a fine line between handsome and repulsive.

Kaitlyn didn't like feeling that way about him, and she tried not to let her reaction show on her face as she smiled. "Hello, Phillip."

"Is everything okay?" he asked anxiously.

"I'm fine. Practically as good as new. I'm not here as a patient. I…came to see a friend."

"Oh, anyone I know?"

"No, I don't think so," she evaded. Glancing at her watch, she said, "I'm sorry to cut this short, but I only have a few minutes before I have to get back to the paper."

"I understand." But something flickered in his dark eyes. Disapproval? Anger? Kaitlyn couldn't quite tell. "I won't keep you. Before I let you go, though, I'd like to ask you something…" He paused, as if suddenly at a loss for words. Then shrugging, he said, "I don't know that many people in town anymore. I haven't had much time to renew old acquaintances since I moved back here. I was wondering…if we could have dinner sometime."

Now it was Kaitlyn who was at a loss for words. He'd taken her completely by surprise, and she didn't know what to say. The last thing she wanted to do was spend an evening with Phillip Becker, and yet she couldn't just turn him down. How rude would that be? Besides, one dinner wouldn't kill her.

She smiled and nodded. "Sure. I'd like that. But…I'm swamped at work right now. Give me a few days to catch up."

"I understand. I'll give you a call next week."

He smiled then, and Kaitlyn was mildly shocked by the transformation. He was full-out handsome when he smiled, and yet there was still something about him that made her want to recoil when he reached out and touched her arm. "I'll talk to you soon."

She waited until he'd disappeared down the hallway, then she turned back to the elevator, wondering what on earth she would find to talk about with Phillip Becker for an entire evening.

She'd worry about that later. Right now she had a date with a dead guy.

The morgue was located in the basement and Kaitlyn knew the procedure. She stepped up to the counter to sign in.

"Kaitlyn?" Dr. Lake had just come out of her office down the hall, and she paused when she saw Kaitlyn. "What are you doing here?"

"I'm here to see you. Do you have a minute?"

"I have a feeling I know what this is about," she said warily. "I'm not sure how much I can help you, but come on back. Word sure travels fast," she muttered as Kaitlyn trailed her back to her office. "I assume you're here about the John Doe that was brought in last night?"

Kaitlyn nodded. "What can you tell me about him?"

"Not much, and anything I do tell you has to be off the record." Dr. Lake went over to the coffeepot behind her desk, poured them each a cup and motioned for Kaitlyn to take a seat. "Sheriff Granger has asked us not to release any information to the public until we can make an ID and notify next of kin. You can't print anything without clearing it with his office."

"Understood." Kaitlyn had a good working relationship with both Dr. Lake and Sheriff Larry Granger. They knew they could trust her, and, consequently, often found themselves revealing more than they'd originally meant to.

Dr. Lake took a sip of her coffee. "The victim is a male Caucasian, probably somewhere in his late forties to mid-fifties."

"Cause of death?"

"He hasn't been autopsied yet, but it appears to be exsanguination. X-rays show that his carotid and jugular were severed."

"His throat was cut?" Kaitlyn winced. "That's…brutal."

"Yeah, it's brutal," Dr. Lake agreed. "And it gets worse."

"What do you mean?"

Dr. Lake got up to close the door. When she came back to her desk, she perched on the edge, dangling one leg as she cradled her coffee cup in both hands. "He was found near an old hunting lodge up by Devil's Canyon."

"Devil's Canyon. That's where…" *I was found,* Kaitlyn started to say, but trailed off as a sudden vision flashed through her head. For just a split second, a building materialized in her head, rustic and seemingly abandoned except for a light gleaming from a front window.

"Kaitlyn? Are you okay?"

She shook off the vision and glanced up at Dr. Lake. "Yeah. I was…just trying to picture the area in my head."

Dr. Lake nodded. "It's pretty remote, and the terrain is rugged this time of year. The killer probably thought the body wouldn't be found until next spring."

"So who found him?"

"A couple of bounty hunters, as I understand it. I guess they were up there looking for the fugitives."

That made sense. Aidan had said that he and his colleague were already in the air searching for Fowler and the others when they got word of her. They'd probably gone back to the area to conduct a more thorough search.

"Do you have any idea how long he'd been out there?"

"Judging from the condition of the body, I'd guess anywhere from forty-eight to seventy-two hours. The nights are getting pretty chilly, especially in the higher elevations, and the cooler temperatures would help slow decomposition. On the other hand, all this rain can accelerate putrification. Do you want to hear about the maggots?"

Kaitlyn's stomach recoiled. She'd been about to take a drink of her coffee, but now she slid the cup away. "Uh, no, that's okay." She stared down at her notes for a moment. "You said earlier that it gets worse. What did you mean by that?"

"The body was buried in a shallow grave, but the rain and wild animals had partially exposed his head and upper torso. His face is severely damaged, including a missing mandible."

Kaitlyn looked up with a frown. "Are you telling me scavengers carried off this poor guy's jaw?"

"Only part of it, and no, I'm not saying animals did it. Unless some scavenger was also able to burn off his fingerprints with acid."

"My God."

Dr. Lake nodded. "Someone went to a lot of trouble to make sure this John Doe wouldn't be identified by his fingerprints or dental records."

Kaitlyn let out a breath. She certainly hadn't expected this when Sherry had sent her over here. From Dr. Lake's description, this was no routine homicide, if there was such a thing. It was sounding more and more like a professional hit.

"What about DNA tests?" she asked.

Dr. Lake shrugged. "That only provides help with identification if you've got something to compare the results to."

"Have you checked the missing person reports?"

"I'm assuming Granger is doing that even as we speak. But last I heard he hadn't turned up anything. There is one thing, though. The x-rays I took showed that the victim was severely injured recently, probably within the last year. He had pins in his right femur and a shattered patella, as well as fractures in his right clavicle and humerus. He also had a lot of scarring on his upper torso. My guess is he was in some sort of accident, most likely a car crash. That could help with the ID."

"I'll do some checking and see what I can find out," Kaitlyn said as she gathered up her notes and pen and stuffed them into her bag.

"If you find out anything, let me know, okay? Somehow it always bothers me when they don't have a name. I don't like thinking of somebody's husband or son or brother lying in the cooler with a blank toe tag."

"I'll let you know," Kaitlyn promised. "And I won't print anything without clearance from Sheriff Granger."

"Thanks."

Dr. Lake stood up to walk her out, and as she opened the door, loud voices drifted down the hall. Two men in dark suits stood at the front desk arguing with one of the orderlies.

"Is there a problem?" Dr. Lake called out.

At the sound of her voice, the young orderly looked up in relief. "Dr. Lake, these two men are with the FBI. They claim—"

As the two men turned, Kaitlyn stepped quickly back into the office. Dr. Lake didn't seem to notice. She hurried down the hall toward the desk.

"You're Dr. Lake?" Kaitlyn heard one of the men ask her.

"I am."

"I'm Special Agent McHenry. This is my partner, Special Agent Clovis. We have a court order authorizing us to take possession of the John Doe that was brought in here last evening."

"But I haven't even autopsied him," Dr. Lake protested.

"Our pathologists will take care of that. But we will need your file on him, including your notes, x-rays, photographs…everything."

"That'll take some time. There's paperwork to be filled out, and I'll have to have someone prepare the body for transit—"

"We'll take care of that, Doctor, if you'll just show us where the cooler is. And one more thing. We'd appreciate the discretion of you and your staff. In fact, it would be better for everyone concerned if you just forget you ever saw this guy."

Chapter Nine

As soon as Kaitlyn got back to the paper, she headed straight for Ken's office. She knocked once, then barely waited for his gruff "Come in" before she flung open the door and strode in.

"I need to talk to you about my assignments…" Her words trailed off when she saw that Allen Cudlow once again had his skinny butt firmly attached to the chair across from Ken's desk.

Crap! Kaitlyn thought. What fresh hell was the man cooking up for her now?

Allen Cudlow had been a thorn in her side for so long now that she barely paid attention to him on most days. He was only a few years older than she, in his late thirties with bad posture, a receding hairline and a sneer that seemed to be permanently affixed to his face.

In the five years she'd worked at the paper, Kaitlyn didn't think she'd run across a single soul who liked the man. He seemed to go out of his way to rub people the wrong way.

Kaitlyn knew very little about his personal life, and had absolutely zero desire to learn more. In fact, the less space Allen Cudlow took up in her brain, the better.

"I'll come back later," she said abruptly.

"No, wait." Ken motioned to the second chair across from his desk. "As a matter of fact, Allen and I have been discussing some assignment changes, and this concerns you."

Kaitlyn frowned. "In what way?"

"Have a seat and we'll talk about it."

Kaitlyn didn't like the sound of that. She hadn't forgotten all the times Cudlow had gone behind her back with Ken's predecessor to sabotage her and she wouldn't put it past him to try to do the same thing with Ken. Luckily, the new editor in chief seemed immune to Cudlow's machinations…unless Cudlow had come up with a new tactic.

It was a little strange—and certainly suspicious—that he hadn't said anything since Kaitlyn had entered the office. Usually, he would have been at her by now, but instead, he seemed content to lean back and wait for her to squirm.

She sat down, folded her arms and sat perfectly still. "What's this about, Ken?"

"Like I said, we're making some changes, and now that you're back, you need to be brought up to speed."

Kaitlyn had a bad feeling these "changes" had something to do with the fact that Cudlow had covered for her at the warden's press conference. If she didn't know better, she'd swear the man had made a pact with the devil to give him control over the weather. But that would be giving him too much credit. He was just a sneaky little opportunist who knew how to get under Kaitlyn's skin. Bigtime.

"What kind of changes?" she asked suspiciously.

"For one thing, I'm axing the Petrov story."

Kaitlyn gasped. "What? Why? Petrov is huge."

"He's too huge," Ken said. "He's got reporters from every major news outlet in the country, including the networks, covering every move he makes. They're all over the guy. There's no way we can compete with that kind of coverage. If we can't offer a unique perspective, then what's the point?"

"But I'm still working on an interview," Kaitlyn said. "Not even the networks have been able to get a sit-down with him."

"If you can pull that off, then you'll get the front page of every newspaper in the country, including this one," Ken said. "But in the meantime, we need to get back to what we do best…covering local news."

Kaitlyn groaned inwardly. She'd attended enough school-board elections and chili cook-offs to last her a lifetime.

Ken sat back and folded his hands behind his head. "If we took a poll in this county, what story do you think would occupy the top spot in order of importance?"

"The flood," Kaitlyn said automatically.

"Normally, yes, but what else do you think is on people's minds these days?"

"The prison break," Cudlow said, and shot Kaitlyn a look.

"Bingo," Ken said. "People are on edge thinking the fugitives could still be in this area. It's all anyone around here can talk about."

Kaitlyn frowned. "It's also national news, just like the Petrov story."

"No, not really. The media is in love with Petrov, and every other story out there, no matter how big, gets overshadowed by this guy." Ken leaned forward, his eyes gleaming. "Which means we can own the fugitive story. The search is being conducted in our own backyard and nobody knows the territory as well as we do."

It was odd, Kaitlyn thought, that Allen Cudlow was still being so silent on the subject. He was up to something.

"I don't want a regurgitation of what comes off the wires," Ken said. "I'm giving you two a chance to do some real investigative reporting. Talk to the feds, the cops, anyone you can think of who might have information regarding the search. I want you chasing down leads, interviewing eyewitnesses, beating the bushes for tidbits the national media might miss. This is our chance to shine, and I expect you both to bust your asses to make me look good. Any questions?"

"Just one." Kaitlyn looked at Ken. "You don't expect us to work together, do you?"

"I expect cooperation and coordination," Ken said sternly. "I don't care what your petty differences were in the past, that's over and done with now. From here on out, we work together as a team."

When hell freezes over, Kaitlyn thought.

ONCE KEN'S MIND WAS made up, there was no dissuading him, and Kaitlyn didn't waste her time trying. A few days ago, she would have jumped at the chance to do the kind of investigative reporting that he was suggesting, and she would have been all over the fugitive piece. She had her own reasons for wanting Boone Fowler caught and sent back to prison, and she would have done everything in her power to make sure that happened.

But working with Allen Cudlow…that put a damper on what would ordinarily have been a huge opportunity for Kaitlyn. She couldn't stand the man, she didn't trust him, and she still had a bad feeling that he had orchestrated the whole thing for some ulterior motive that she didn't yet understand.

She knew one thing, though. Experience had taught her that Cudlow would stab her in the back at the first opportunity. Her best defense was to get out ahead of him on the story.

To that end, she put in a call to Eden. When she couldn't reach her at the office, Kaitlyn tried her cell phone.

"Eden McClain," she responded curtly.

"Eden, it's Kaitlyn. Bad time?"

"The new poll numbers just came out and we lost ground on almost every issue, so I'm not exactly having a great day," Eden grumbled.

"Should I call back later?"

"No, of course, not. I don't mean to take my bad mood out on you. I'm glad to hear from you. I take it this means you're doing okay?"

"I'm fine," Kaitlyn said as she unlocked a desk drawer and took out a CD. It was labeled MMFAFA, and she'd kept it under lock and key for the past five years. "I'm back at work…which is why I'm calling. I need a favor."

"Name it."

"I'm working on a story about Boone Fowler's escape from the Fortress, and I'd like to get Governor Gilbert's reaction."

"He issued a statement almost immediately," Eden said. "I can fax you a copy if you want."

"No, I already have his public statement. I want something more. Something no one else has."

"I hope you're not asking for an interview," Eden said. "Because that would be impossible. We're entering the final stages of the campaign, and every moment from here to Election Day is already packed."

"It doesn't have to be a sit-down interview," Kaitlyn said. "We could do it over the phone. Wouldn't take more than five minutes."

Eden sighed. "You don't ask for much, do you? Does this mean you're giving up on the Petrov interview?"

"Not if you've got something for me," Kaitlyn said quickly.

"I'm doing my best, but I'm not a miracle worker. Petrov has more handlers and bodyguards than the POTUS. I can't get near him. But I think I can at least get you an introduction."

"I'm listening."

"You've heard about the governor's big masquerade ball at the Denning mansion next weekend, right?"

Who hadn't? It was a huge event that Eden had orchestrated to give her boss several crucial days of saturated coverage. While his opponent schlepped his way from one bad barbeque to another, Peter Gilbert would be seen on the evening news and on the front pages of every newspaper in the state looking statesmanlike and regal as he hobnobbed with the rich and famous.

"We had originally planned it as a fundraising event, but the governor's decided to donate the proceeds instead to a children's-relief fund in Lukinburg. The prince and his sister have agreed to come, and they've requested that we only invite a few members of the press so that the evening doesn't turn into a circus. I can get you in and I can try to get you an introduction with Petrov, but that's the best I can do. Take it or leave it."

"I'll take it," Kaitlyn said, jotting the date on her calendar. "And the governor?"

"I'll try to get you a few minutes alone with him as well. But, Kaitlyn...I'm going to need something in return."

"What is it?"

"Immediately after the ball, the governor is heading out on his whistle-stop tour of the state. The reporters who are invited to the ball will also be allowed to accompany him on the train trip, and, in light of some of the hostile press he's been receiving lately, I'd like to make sure there's at least one friendly face in the crowd."

Kaitlyn frowned. "What exactly are you asking me to do?"

"I'm not asking you to slant your coverage in favor of Peter," Eden assured her. "I wouldn't do that. I just want you to give him a fair shake."

"Agreed," Kaitlyn said. "So how do I get into this shindig anyway? With Petrov and his sister in attendance, the security will be a nightmare."

"I'll send you a ticket," Eden said. "And I'll make sure your name is on the guest list. All you have to do is show up with your ID."

They chatted for a few more minutes, and then Kaitlyn hung up. She sat for a moment staring at the disc she'd recovered from her drawer. All the notes and research material she'd accumulated five years ago on the MMFAFA was contained on that disc, but after Jenny's disappearance, Kaitlyn had lost her stomach for the story.

With Boone Fowler's escape, some of the information she'd uncovered five years ago had suddenly become relevant again. But did she really want to go digging up all that old pain and guilt? Did she really want to invite the ghosts of her past back into her life?

Out of the corner of her eye, she saw Allen Cudlow approach her desk. Slipping the disc back into the drawer, she locked her desk and pocketed the key.

Glancing up with a frown, she said coldly, "What do you want, Allen?"

"You heard Ken. He wants us to work together on this story, so I thought it might be time we came to some kind of an understanding."

His new conciliatory attitude didn't fool Kaitlyn one bit. Beneath the Dockers, loafers and blazer, he was still the same old Cudlow.

Even though she couldn't stand the man, his choice of attire always amused her. He would have looked more at home on an Ivy League campus than the wilds of Montana. Kaitlyn wondered if the man even owned a pair of boots. She was pretty sure he'd never been on a horse.

"So what do you say? You want to bury the hatchet?"

"Considering that you've tried your damnedest to get me fired for the past five years, I don't think you want to know where I'd like to bury the hatchet," Kaitlyn said.

"Even if it's for the good of the paper?"

She narrowed her eyes. "You don't fool me. Two days ago you couldn't stand the sight of me. Somehow I don't think your feelings have changed that quickly just because Ken wants us to work together."

Something flickered in his eyes as he planted his hands on her desk and leaned forward. "You're right. My feelings about you haven't changed. I still think you're a spoiled little rich girl trying to impress her important daddy."

"Is that so?"

"Yeah, that's so. You couldn't cut it back East so you came out here."

"That's funny, because last time I checked, you and I work for the same paper. I don't exactly see the suits at the *Times* or the *Post* beating a path to your door, either."

Cudlow's face went tight with anger. "There's one big difference between you and me. I got this job on merit, not as a favor to my hotshot father."

"Where are you talking about?"

He smirked. "What? You didn't know that's how you got the job? The publisher owed Logan Wilson a favor and he called it in. For you."

Kaitlyn clenched her teeth. "You're lying."

"Why don't you call Daddy and ask him?"

"You know what, Allen? If what you say is true, then I can understand why you might resent me. But what I don't understand is why you feel so threatened by me."

"Threatened? By you? I don't think so."

"But you are. Especially when I started working on my investigative piece about local involvement in the MMFAFA. If I thought about it long enough and hard enough, I just might start to wonder about the timing of your animosity."

Cudlow leaned in even closer, his eyes going dark with fury. "You still have no idea who you're dealing with, do you?"

"Get out of my face, Allen."

He straightened and glared down at her. "Before this is over, you're going to regret making me your enemy."

"That almost sounds like a threat."

"Take it any way you want." He turned and stalked off.

"Ooh, I'm so scared," Kaitlyn muttered as she watched him leave the room.

"Kaitlyn?"

She jumped, her hand flying to her heart as she whirled. "Good grief, don't you know better than to sneak up on a person like that?"

"Sorry," Aidan said. "I didn't mean to startle you. The receptionist said I could come on back."

Kaitlyn glanced around him to where Sherry was craning her neck to get a better look at his backside. "Yeah, I'll just bet she did."

"It seems I've come at a bad time." Aidan paused. "What was that all about, if you don't mind my asking?"

"Oh…nothing. Just an editorial disagreement." Kaitlyn stopped to draw a breath. Her heart was still pounding, but not so much from being startled now.

Aidan Campbell was looking better than ever. Dressed in faded jeans and a black sweater, he was about as hot as a man could get. "So…what are you doing here?"

"We need to talk." He glanced around the small newsroom. Everyone had stopped what they were doing to stare at him, although they pretended to be busy when he glanced their way. "Could we go somewhere more private?"

"Uh, yeah, that's probably a good idea." Kaitlyn grabbed her purse and headed out of the newsroom.

As she breezed through the reception area, she said over her shoulder, "Sherry, I'm going out for a little while. If you need me you can call my cell phone."

Out on the street, she said, "We could go to the diner if you feel like coffee."

"Coffee sounds good, but I don't want anyone overhearing what I have to say."

Kaitlyn's heart skipped a beat. "That sounds...ominous."

He nodded as he slipped on his sunglasses. "Not to sound melodramatic, but it could be a matter of life and death."

Chapter Ten

Five minutes later, they were at Kaitlyn's apartment. Aidan had barely said a word to her on the way over, and now as Kaitlyn unlocked her front door, she realized how nervous she felt. What could he want to talk to her about that was so important? So…ominous? A matter of life and death?

Finally getting the door open, she stepped inside and motioned for Aidan to enter.

"Excuse the mess." She grabbed up newspapers on the way to the kitchen. "Make yourself at home while I put on some coffee."

As Kaitlyn puttered about the kitchen, she kept sneaking glances at Aidan. Her living room was small, and he seemed to fill up the entire space. It wasn't so much his height or those broad shoulders, but the man had *presence.* He dominated every room he entered, no matter the size, making it impossible to focus on anyone but him.

And being alone with him in her apartment certainly did nothing to calm her nerves, Kaitlyn realized as she dropped one thing after another.

Finally she had everything ready, and she carried a tray to her dining-room table. "You take your coffee black, right?"

"Black is fine." He came over to the table to join her.

Kaitlyn handed him a cup, then poured one for her. Sitting down at the table, she placed a plate of oatmeal cookies her landlady had brought over that morning on the table between them.

One brow lifted slightly. "What, no Hungry Man Special this morning?"

She appreciated his attempt at humor, but it fell a little flat. "I don't eat like that every morning." She waited a heartbeat, then said, "What did you want to talk to me about? It sounds serious."

He immediately sobered. "Before I get

into it, I want to ask you something, and I'd like you be completely candid with me."

Kaitlyn frowned. "Why would you assume I wouldn't be candid?"

"I don't assume anything. But I need to know that you've told me everything you remember about your accident." His expression never changed, but his eyes seemed to darken. "Including whether or not it was an accident."

Kaitlyn looked at him aghast. "What? Of course, it was an accident. What else could it have been? You don't think I jumped into that ravine, do you?"

"Just tell me if you've remembered anything else."

She shrugged. "No…not really. I've had some flashes, but nothing concrete and nothing that makes any real sense. But…" She trailed off and glanced out the window.

"But what?" he pressed.

Her attention was still on the window, but she couldn't seem to focus on anything outside. "It's like…I know there's something I should remember, but I can't. The memory is *right there,* but I just can't grasp it." She turned back to Aidan. "Why do I get the feeling that you know what that something is?"

"I don't. Not really. What I do know is that a body was found near Devil's Canyon yesterday." He watched her closely, waiting for her reaction.

"I know. When I heard that it was two bounty hunters who'd found the body, I wondered if one of them was you."

Now it was his turn to be surprised. "You already know about this?"

She gave him a tense little smile. "You forget, I'm an investigative reporter, and I have a lot of contacts in this town. The pathologist who was scheduled to do the autopsy is a friend of mine."

Aidan sat back and frowned. "Sheriff Granger wanted to keep a lid on the investigation until they could ID the body. I doubt he's going to appreciate a leak."

"He doesn't have anything to worry about from me," Kaitlyn assured him. "Dr. Lake and I have an understanding. I won't print anything about the John Doe or the investigation until I get Sheriff Granger's okay. But it's out of his hands now that the FBI has taken charge of the investigation."

"The FBI?" Aidan's tone sharpened. "What are you talking about?"

"Two FBI agents came to the morgue while I was there yesterday. They had a court order authorizing them to take possession of the body. But Aidan—" Kaitlyn gave him a warning look "—that's off the record, too."

He didn't seem to hear her. "Why would the feds be interested in this John Doe?" he mused.

"That's the money question," Kaitlyn agreed. "But you found the body so you must know this is no ordinary John Doe. The man's face was mutilated and his fingerprints were burned off to keep him from being identified. We're not talking a run-of-the-mill homicide here."

Aidan's jaw hardened. "It's worse than that. We found the body near Devil's Canyon, buried behind an old hunting lodge. *Devil's Canyon,* Kaitlyn. Do you get what I'm saying?"

Her heart quickened at the look on his face, the note of something in his voice that might have been an indictment. Then her face went red with anger even as her blood turned cold. "What exactly are you accusing me of here, Aidan?"

"I'm not accusing you of anything. I'm trying to find out what the hell happened up on that mountain."

"From me? Why in the world would you assume I'd know something about this man's murder? Just because you found me near Devil's Canyon doesn't mean anything. It's just a weird coincidence or something. This guy could have already been dead when I got there. His body could have been buried for—"

"Days? Weeks? Try forty-eight to seventy-two hours. It was a fresh kill, Kaitlyn. Trust me, I know these things."

A shiver snaked up her spine at his words. She hadn't given much thought to Aidan's past. There hadn't been time. But here they were, alone, discussing matters of murder.

When he reached over to take her arm, Kaitlyn jumped a little.

He didn't remove his hand. Instead his grasp tightened. "If you've remembered anything, anything at all, you need to tell me."

Kaitlyn didn't much care for his tone. She wasn't the type of woman to meekly submit to a man's demands. In fact, more often than not, a note of authority brought out the rebel in her. She thought about telling Aidan where he could stuff his accusations, but another side of her, a more reasonable side, decided that it might be smart if she found out what was going on, too.

She nodded. "All right, there is something. When I first heard that the body had been found near Devil's Canyon, I had a flash... this image of an old, rustic building with a light in the window." She shrugged. "I have no idea if it's a real memory or not."

"Oh, I think the memory is real, all right."

She glanced up. "How do you know?"

"You said when you left the highway after you were stranded, you headed due north, toward Eagle Falls. If you stayed on course, you would have seen that lodge."

She frowned. "So?"

"The canyon is to the west. It runs parallel to the highway. For some reason, you veered off course."

"If you're asking for an explanation, I

can't give you one," she said defensively. "Like I've already said a hundred times, I don't remember how I fell."

"Then we have to find a way to make you remember." Aidan's eyes burned into hers. "Because I think you witnessed that murder, Kaitlyn."

She gasped. *"What?"*

"We found blood inside the lodge. And I found this buried in the mud outside the front window." He pulled a cell phone from his pocket and handed it to her. "Do you recognize it?"

"It looks like mine," she admitted. "I thought I lost it when I fell."

"I don't think so. I think when you stumbled upon that lodge you decided to check it out before you went inside. Maybe you heard something. I don't know what drew you to the window, but I'm guessing whatever you saw made you run."

"You think I was trying to get away from the killer?" Kaitlyn's heart was beating so hard now she could hardly breathe. Could it be true? Had she witnessed a murder? But...how could she forget something like that?

Suddenly, something Phillip Becker told her about PTSD came rushing back to her. *"Any fearful trauma can produce symptoms. Think of it as the aftershock of an extremely threatening event."*

Kaitlyn had assumed the fall had triggered the hallucination she'd experienced in the hospital and the acute sense of danger she'd been unable to shake in her own home. But what if something far more sinister had been the cause?

"Kaitlyn."

She jumped again.

"You saw the killer. His identity is locked somewhere in your memory. I think your subconscious has been trying to tell you who he is."

"What do you mean?" she asked fearfully.

"You told me you had a hallucination while you were in the hospital."

"But that's all it was, Aidan. A hallucination. It wasn't real."

"But why Boone Fowler? I know what you told me," he said quickly, suppressing her argument. "He was on your mind because you were headed to that press conference and because you'd seen his picture on TV. I think it was more than that. Like I said, I think your subconscious is trying to tell you something."

She fell silent for a moment, thinking about everything he'd told her. "Is that why you're here?" she finally asked. "Because you think I know something about Boone Fowler?"

"I'm here because I want to help you."

"Help me how?"

"You're in danger, Kaitlyn. You have to see that."

"No, I don't," she said stubbornly. "Even if I did witness this murder and even if Boone Fowler and his men were responsible…why would they care? They're wanted fugitives. If they're caught, they'll be sent back to prison for the rest of their natural lives. Why would they take a chance on getting apprehended just to come after me?"

"That's a good question." Aidan got up and began to pace. "I keep coming back to the fact that, as you said, this was no ordinary homicide. They went to a great deal of trouble to make sure the victim wouldn't be easily identified. Why would they do that if they weren't concerned about being caught? And now the feds are involved. There's something going on here that we don't understand, and it looks to me like you've stumbled right smack into the middle of it."

Kaitlyn put a hand to her mouth, then dropped it to her lap. She couldn't seem to sit still. "Even if everything you say is true, it's not your problem, Aidan. You're not a cop. You're a bounty hunter. Now why are you really here?"

He stopped pacing and stared down at her. "Is it so hard to believe that I just want to help you?"

"No, of course, it's not. You've already saved my life, and you have no idea how grateful I am. But…you don't owe me anything. If I'm in danger, then I can go to the police. Or the FBI."

"But would you?" Aidan paused, as if choosing his words carefully. "What if you went to the FBI, told them what you know, or what you think you know, and they wanted to put you into protected custody? Would you go along with that?"

She shrugged.

"I thought not."

She got to her feet. "And what exactly are you going to do, Aidan? Move in here with me? Follow me around twenty-four hours a day? I'm not your responsibility and I can't help wondering what your motive is in all this."

"My motive? What the hell are you talking about?"

"You're a bounty hunter. Boone Fowler has a price on his head. All you need to draw him out is a little bait, right?"

Aidan looked as if he wanted to deny her charge, then glancing away, he ran a hand through his hair. "Look, I'm not going to lie to you. Yeah, I want to get Boone Fowler. By any means necessary. If I can save your life in the process, so much the better. Do you have a problem with that?"

She sat back down. "No. I'm glad you laid it all out like that. Honesty is certainly the best policy."

"I'm glad you feel that way, because there's something else I need to know." He came back over and stood in front of her.

"Before Boone Fowler escaped, you went out to the prison to see him on more than one occasion."

"How do you know about that?"

"Colonel Murphy has a lot of friends in a lot of places. Why did you go to see Fowler?"

"I'm a reporter. I wanted an interview."

"Did he give you one?"

"No, he refused to see me, just as he did every other reporter who went out to the Fortress."

"Then why did you keep going? The log showed you went out there on five consecutive weekends. Why?"

"Because I kept hoping he'd change his mind."

Aidan squatted, staring directly into her eyes. When she tried to glance away, he took her chin and turned her face back to his. "And that's the only reason?"

"OH, AIDAN." Kaitlyn put her hand up to his face, then dropped it almost at once. "You can't seriously think I had anything to do with Fowler's escape. That is what you're implying, isn't it?"

Her reaction wasn't at all what Aidan had expected. Anger, yes. Denial, maybe. But the look of disappointment in her eyes was a little hard to take. "I just want to know why you were you so persistent, that's all."

"Okay, I'll tell you." Very subtly, she removed his hand from her chin. "I wanted to ask him where he buried Jenny Peltier's body. I know he killed her, but without remains, I'll never be able to prove it." Resentment flashed briefly in her eyes. "Satisfied?"

Aidan drew a breath. He hadn't expected that, either.

She pushed her chair back and stood. "I need a little breathing room if you don't mind."

"Sorry." He straightened and moved away from the table.

She clasped her hands in front of her, seemingly at a loss for a moment. "It started just before the bombing of the federal building here in Montana five years ago," she said hesitantly. She picked up the tray from the table and carried it into the kitchen, as if she needed something to do. She stood at the sink for a moment, then glanced back at him. "I need to tell you something. Something about me. About the way I was back then. I'm not making excuses for what happened, I just… need you to know the whole story."

Aidan nodded. "I'm listening."

The words seemed to pour out of her then, as if she'd had her story bottled up for far too long. She leaned against the kitchen counter and folded her arms. "My first job as a journalist was with the *Washington Sun.* I was one of their rising stars, a female Logan Wilson, they called me. They groomed me, polished me, promoted me, and pretty soon I found myself in way over my head. I…did some things I never thought I would do just to try to keep myself afloat. I won't bore you with the details," she said with a shrug. "Suffice it to say, I was fired and humiliated and I came back here to lick my wounds."

"Go on."

"I finally landed a job with the *Monitor.* It wasn't anything like what I'd been doing for the *Sun,* but it was a job, and I was in no position to be picky. And I told myself that, even working for a small-town paper, I could build a name for myself if I worked hard enough. But I wasn't very patient, and I had something to prove. To the editor who fired me, to my father, but mostly to myself. I needed a story. Something big.

"Around that time, I was starting to hear a lot of talk about the Montana Militia for a Free America. I'd been hearing rumors about how they liked to recruit from small towns in the state, and I decided to do an investigative piece on local involvement. But my editor shot me down. He said a story like that was beyond my scope, but if I wanted to do some research for one of his more seasoned reporters, he'd think about it."

"What did you do?"

She shrugged. "I continued to investigate on my own, of course."

"Why does that not surprise me?" Aidan muttered.

"A few weeks later, a woman named Jenny Peltier came to see me. We'd been best friends in high school. We were the same age, but she was almost like a younger sister to me. She'd had a difficult home life, an abusive father, an alcoholic mother. She'd lost her brother a few years back, and his death had devastated her. He was the only one in her family who really cared about her, and she never got over losing him. She was needy and vulnerable, and I had taken her under my wing. But we drifted apart when I went off to college. When I moved back to Ponderosa a few years later, I tried to see her, but she was always too busy. I didn't think much of it, but when she came to see me that night, I realized how much things had changed between us. She was a completely different person. Hard, bitter, cold. So cold. I couldn't get over it."

"What did she want?"

"She said she'd heard I'd been asking questions about the MMFAFA, and she warned me to back off."

Aidan lifted a brow. "What reason did she give you?"

"She said I was poking my nose into places it didn't belong, and I could end up very, very sorry."

"She threatened you?"

"More or less."

"What did you do after that?" Aidan gave her a skeptical look. "Wait, let me guess. You continued to investigate."

"Of course. Wouldn't you?"

"Probably," he admitted grudgingly.

"Anyway, she came back to see me a few days later, and this time, she was like the Jenny I remembered from high school. She was scared to death, and she said she had nowhere else to turn. She showed me the tattoo on her arm, a burning flag, and told me that she'd been recruited into the Militia shortly after I'd left for college. I was appalled. Devastated. I couldn't believe it, and yet, it made an awful kind of sense. Her brother joined the army right after high school. He was killed fighting for something he believed in, but Jenny didn't see it that way. Her stepfather had always railed against the government, and after Chase's death, Jenny started listening to him. She came to believe that her brother had died because his own country betrayed him. I knew she had a lot of conflicted emotions about Chase's death, but I never thought she'd be seduced by the likes of Boone Fowler. I still believe she was somehow coerced into joining the militia, but I guess I'll never know for sure. When I asked her how she'd gotten involved, she implied someone we knew had recruited her, but she wouldn't name names. All she'd say was that something big was in the works. Something that terrified her. She'd overheard a discussion about bomb-making."

Aidan said nothing, but his gut tightened.

"I told her that we needed to go to the police or the FBI, but she was too frightened. She said I had no idea who or what I was dealing with. There were people involved in the militia who had a lot of power. She didn't want to go to the authorities because she didn't trust them."

"What did you do?"

"I wanted to get her away from the group, but I also knew that we had to try to find out what Boone Fowler had planned. So…I sent her back in."

"You did what?"

Kaitlyn closed her eyes briefly. "You heard me. I sent her back in and that was the last time I ever saw her. Two days later, the federal building was bombed."

Aidan scrubbed a hand down his face. "And you think Fowler killed her."

Kaitlyn nodded. "I'm certain of it. I just can't prove it."

"Did you go to the police after the bombing?"

"I talked to the police and to the FBI, but without a body, their hands were tied. All they had to go on was what I'd told them. Besides, the feds already had Fowler for the bombing. They didn't need to charge him with a separate homicide to put him away for life. After I gave my initial statement, I never heard from them again."

Aidan turned away, rubbing the back of his neck. "And you never found out who recruited her?"

"No. After she disappeared, I didn't have the stomach to pursue it anymore. Boone Fowler was in prison. It didn't seem to matter so I stopped asking questions. And besides, I didn't trust myself. I'd made two bad mistakes—one of them fatal—in the pursuit of a story. I decided to play it safe."

Aidan stopped pacing. "Until now."

She came out of the kitchen then and

walked over to the table, running her finger-tips lightly across the surface. "I might have gone on indefinitely, content to cover local politics and the occasional meth bust, but all of a sudden, not one, but *three,* huge stories landed in my lap. Any one of them—Petrov, the prison break, even the John Doe—is the kind of story an investigative reporter would kill to sink her teeth into." She looked at Aidan. "For the past few days, I've been re-minded of what I've been missing all these years, and now, I don't think I can go back to school-board elections and cattle rustlings. I don't think I can play it safe anymore."

"So it's on to bigger and better things," Aidan said.

She nodded. "I don't even know why I'm telling you all this except…if you really want to play the protector, that means we'll be spending a lot of time together. Yesterday when you kissed me…" She trailed off with a wince. "I guess what I'm trying to say is that I'm not available. And now that I have said it, it sounds incredibly presumptuous and conceited of me."

Aidan went over and placed his hands on

her shoulders. When she tilted her head toward his, it was all he could do not to kiss her again, but timing was everything and this was mostly definitely not the right time. "You don't have to worry about that," he said. "I'm not looking for any kind of relationship."

"You're not?"

Was that disappointment or relief he saw in her eyes?

"I want to help you, Kaitlyn. I want to protect you if I can, and yeah, I want to get Boone Fowler. But that's all. No strings attached."

She moistened her lips and nodded. "Okay. If that's the case, then I think I should get something out of this, too."

Aidan lifted a brow. "Aren't you?"

She smiled, her confidence suddenly back full force. "You want Boone Fowler, right? Well, I want something, too."

Aidan's gaze narrowed. "What?"

"An exclusive, including interviews with both you and Cameron Murphy."

He dropped his hands from her shoulders. "I'm trying to save your life here."

"And make a killing in the bargain. Which I don't begrudge you for, by the way." She shrugged. "I gave you my terms. Take them or leave them."

Chapter Eleven

"So for the privilege of saving her life, we're supposed to reward her with an exclusive interview." Murphy sat back in his chair and gave Aidan a dubious glare. "She sounds like a real piece of work."

"She has her moments," Aidan agreed as he took a seat across from Murphy's desk. "Actually, though, I think you'd probably like her. She's got a lot of guts."

"Well, she's going to need them if what you suspect is true." Murphy paused. "However, I'm not so sure she should be our problem at this point. We're not running a bodyguard service here, Campbell."

"I know that. But I think she's very much our problem. You're the one who told me to keep an eye on her in the first place. She may not be able to lead us to Fowler, but she sure as hell can help draw him out."

"*If* what you suspect is true. And that's still a big if. We don't have proof that Fowler and his goons committed that murder or that Kaitlyn Wilson witnessed it. You're basing your assumptions on a hallucination she had in the hospital following a traumatic fall."

"What about the cell phone I found?"

Murphy lifted one shoulder. "It's just one piece of the puzzle. Doesn't prove anything."

"But we can't afford to ignore it," Aidan insisted.

"Besides, either way, she can still be an asset to us. She grew up here and she knows a lot of people in the area. Without her, we wouldn't have known so quickly that the FBI had confiscated that body, and now your contact has all but confirmed that the feds are also looking into a possible link to Fowler." He paused. "If my hunch is right, Colonel, Kaitlyn witnessed that murder. She saw the victim and she saw the killer, and that makes her a target. Whether or not Boone Fowler is connected, I can't just leave her hanging out to dry on this one."

"That was some speech, Campbell. And it leaves me wondering just what the hell *your* connection is to this woman."

Aidan frowned. "What do you mean?"

"Are you falling for her?" Murphy asked bluntly.

Aidan didn't much care for the question, but he answered it anyway. "I hardly know her, but even if I did have feelings for her, how would that be relevant? It wouldn't change the circumstances."

Murphy sat forward. "It's relevant because when I found you six months ago, you were still grieving for a woman you'd been in love with for years. You'd planned to marry her. I haven't forgotten what her death did you, and I doubt that you have, either."

Elena's death had affected Aidan far more profoundly than even Murphy realized, but he had no intention of getting into all that now. "Elena has nothing to do with this."

"Are you sure about that? When you look at Kaitlyn Wilson, are you seeing *her,* or are you seeing a substitute for Elena?"

Aidan's jaw tightened with sudden anger.

"With all due respect, Colonel, you don't know what the hell you're talking about."

"I know that after Elena Sanchez died, you were hell-bent on destroying yourself out of guilt. You don't get over something like that overnight. Sometimes you don't ever get over it."

Aidan's relationship with Elena had been torturous and complicated; what he felt for Kaitlyn was simple. He wanted to protect her. That was it.

He glanced at Murphy. "There's nothing I wouldn't do for you, Colonel. You've saved my hide more times than I want to remember, and I think you know that I'd gladly lay down my life for you. But my personal life is none of your damn business."

Murphy lifted one brow slightly. "I agree, so long as it doesn't interfere with your judgment or your job."

"It won't."

"All right," Murphy said with a curt nod. "Then go get this out of your system. Do what you have to do to feed this savior complex you seem to have, but when this is over with, you make damn sure you still have your head screwed on straight. No more death wishes, Campbell."

Aidan said nothing. He got up to leave, but at the door, he paused and glanced back. "It's pretty ironic, you know."

"What is?"

"That lecture you just gave me." Aidan nodded to the picture of Murphy's wife and daughter on his desk. "If you hadn't let your personal life interfere with your work, none of us would even be here right now."

KAITLYN HAD LIVED alone for so long that she couldn't get used to having someone in her apartment. Her place was so small that she and Aidan kept bumping into each other. And, of course, her attraction to him was like an elephant in the room. She finally went to bed early just so she wouldn't have to deal with it.

But she couldn't sleep. In spite of her exhaustion, she couldn't settle down. She was too aware of Aidan's presence even with a wall dividing them. She could hear every little move he made. When he turned on the shower. When he opened the refrigerator door. She even imagined that she could hear him breathing, and when all was finally quiet in the apartment, she wondered if he was lying on her sofa, staring at the ceiling, the way she was.

In frustration, she rolled over her, punched her pillow and willed herself to sleep. Finally, after what seemed like hours, she drifted off, only to awaken with a start, her heart pounding in terror.

Someone was sitting on the edge of her bed, and she started to scream, but Aidan said softly, "Hey, it's me. You were having a nightmare."

Her heart still racing, Kaitlyn lifted herself on her elbows. It was dark in her room, but she could see Aidan quite clearly. The sight of him shirtless left her even more breathless.

"You were talking in your sleep," he said.

"I was?" She ran a hand through her mussed hair. "What did I say?"

"I couldn't make it out, but you seemed distressed. I thought I should wake you up."

"Thanks." She glanced at the bedside clock. It was only a little after eleven. She hadn't been asleep that long.

"Do you want to talk about it?" Aidan asked softly.

"What, the dream? I'm not sure I even remember." But no sooner were the words out of her mouth than images of a man tied to a chair flashed through her head. He was hurt and she could hear him babbling uncontrollably.

Kaitlyn gasped and clutched Aidan's arm. "I think I just dreamed about the murder."

He nodded, as if not the least bit surprised that she would do so. "Tell me everything you remember."

"I'm not sure how much I can remember, but there was a man. He was tied to a chair, and he was hurt and bleeding. He kept saying something over and over, but I couldn't understand him. I think he was speaking German."

"Can you remember anything he said? What did the words sound like?"

"It's been a long time since I had high-school German, but it was something like, *'Gotthilfe mich. Gotthilfe uns alle, wenn Sie gelingen.'*"

"'God help me. God help us all if you succeed,'" Aidan translated.

Kaitlyn put trembling fingertips to her lips. "What do you think that means?"

Aidan shook his head. "I don't know. Can you remember anything else? Think, Kaitlyn. What did this man look like?"

"Dark hair, middle-aged. He was big, but not overweight, just muscular."

"Was anyone with him?"

"The killer you mean?" Kaitlyn paused. "I don't know. That's all I can remember—"

But it wasn't. Suddenly she had another image. The man's head being jerked back. A knife slicing across his throat. And then blood everywhere...

"Oh, my God," she whispered.

Aidan's grasp tightened on her arm. "What is it, Kaitlyn?"

Nausea rose to her throat, and she clapped a hand across her mouth. "I'm going to be sick." Sliding off the bed, she dove for the bathroom. Slamming the door shut, she fell on her knees in front of the toilet.

When she was finally finished, she rose on wobbly legs to wash her face and brush her teeth. Then she staggered back out to the bedroom.

Aidan glanced up worriedly. "Are you all right?"

She wrapped her arms around her middle. "I guess so. There was so much blood, Aidan. It was awful."

"I know." He drew her down to the bed. "Try to relax for a minute. I need to call Murphy and tell him what you've remembered."

"But we don't know for sure that it was a memory," she protested. "Maybe it was nothing more than a dream. My subconscious could have conjured up that guy from what I learned at the morgue."

"Maybe. I need to let Murphy know just the same. I'll be right back."

As he left the room, Kaitlyn got up and followed him out. She stood at the door and watched as he picked up his cell phone and lifted it to his ear.

He glanced in her direction, but he was so distracted by his phone conversation that Kaitlyn wasn't sure he even saw her.

She was all too aware of him. Even after the distress of the dream, she couldn't help appreciating the way he looked all shirtless and shoeless, his only attire a pair of sexy, low-riding jeans.

He looked like a god or a movie star, she thought. Or one of those underwear models in the Abercrombie & Fitch catalogs. He had huge biceps and broad shoulders, but the rest of him was all lean and sinewy. A tapered waist and abs so cut she could see the ripple even in the darkness. She wanted to run her hands over those muscles. Feel that lean hard body against hers…

She drew a deep breath. And only a moment ago she'd been dreaming about murder. So nice to know she had her priorities straight.

Aidan hung up the phone and placed it on the end table near the sofa. Then straightening, he noticed her in the doorway.

"I wasn't eavesdropping," she said quickly, which was true. She hadn't heard a word he said. "I just came to get some water."

He headed for the kitchen. "I'll get it for you."

"I can get it. You don't have to wait on

me," she protested, when he beat her to the kitchen. "I'm not helpless."

He came back over to where she stood and took her hand. Lifting it up, he pointed to the scrapes that were scabbing over and the shredded nails that she'd trimmed down to the quick. "Those are not the hands of someone helpless," he said. "You forget that I've seen you in action. I know exactly what you're capable of. I'm not trying to offend you. I'm just trying to be nice to you. I would expect the same from you if I'd been the one upchucking my last two meals."

"Three," she muttered. But she didn't say another word as he went into the kitchen and filled her a glass of water.

When he brought it to her, she took a few sips then set the glass aside.

"Tell me again why you're here, Aidan."

He cocked his head with a frown. "Didn't we already have this conversation?"

"Yes." She folded her arms. "But I still don't quite understand why you're here.

"What is you're fishing for, Kaitlyn? What do you want me to say?"

His bluntness angered her at first, and then

she realized he was right. She was fishing for something. She just didn't know what. "I feel empty and restless and...I don't know why."

"You're dead on your feet, that's why," he said sternly. "You need to sleep."

"I *can't* sleep. I...don't want to be alone."

"You won't be alone. I'll be right in here on that sofa. If you need anything, all you have to do is call out."

"Maybe I didn't make myself clear," Kaitlyn said softly. "I don't want to be *alone*."

His eyes darkened as he stared down at her. "Are you saying what I think you're saying?"

"There is such a thing as comfort sex, right?"

"I'm not very good at comforting," he finally said.

"What are you good at?" She put out a tentative hand and traced it along his washboard abs.

He sucked in a breath and caught her hand. "You sure you want to start this party?"

His eyes burned into hers, and now it was Kaitlyn who caught her breath. To answer him, she lifted her hand to cup the back of his neck and pull his head down to hers. She kissed him as she'd never kissed anyone before. Except for Aidan.

He drew back in surprise. But he didn't say a word. Instead he stared at her for a moment before lowering his head to kiss her back, deep and hard and without one ounce of comfort.

He wrapped his arms around her waist, lifted her up and kept right on kissing her. He kissed her all the way across the room to the sofa, and then he dropped her on the cushions and lowered himself over her.

He studied her features in the darkness. "You're sure this is what you want?"

"It was my idea, remember?" Kaitlyn tangled her fingers in his short hair and yanked him closer. "You don't have a problem with assertive women, do you?"

"No problem at all. We can even switch positions if you want."

He started to turn them so that she was on top, but Kaitlyn rolled the wrong way and ended up on the floor on her back.

Aidan didn't miss a beat. He rolled off the couch on top of her and, bracing his hands on the floor, kissed her again. Then he slid his arms beneath her and this time rolled her on top of him.

He tugged at the hem of her pajama top. "You're wearing too many clothes," he muttered.

Before he could unbutton her top, Kaitlyn whipped it over her head and flung it aside.

The lights were still off, but she knew he could see her as clearly as she could see him. She wasn't embarrassed by her body. She worked out, and she didn't even mind when Aidan seemed fixated on her breasts.

"Wow," he muttered. "I'm impressed." And to show her, he cupped them in his hands, and then rose to taste first one then the other with his mouth and tongue.

The sensations storming through her felt almost too good, and she pushed him back against the floor and flattened herself against him. While she kissed him, he slipped his hands inside her pajamas and splayed his hands over her buttocks, pressing her so tightly against him that she could feel his arousal through his jeans.

"Wow," she whispered against his mouth. "Now, I'm impressed. Please tell me—" she kissed him again "—you brought…" another kiss "—a condom."

"Wallet. End table."

Of course, he had a condom, Kaitlyn thought. Not because he'd anticipated what was happening between them, but because a man like him would always be prepared. He probably had women throwing themselves at him all the time. Just as she was doing at that very moment.

Kaitlyn slid off him and scrambled for his wallet. It fell open, and in the dim light from the street, she caught a glimpse of a woman's photo. Then his phone rang, startling her, and she snatched her hand back as if she'd spied a snake. She shot Aidan a glance. "You don't want to get that, do you?"

He rose on his elbows, his focus glued to hers. "I'd better. It could be important."

She tossed him the phone, then reached for her pajama top. He grabbed it out of her hand and flung it over his shoulder as he answered the phone. Then he grabbed for her.

"Campbell," he all but barked as he lay back on the floor with Kaitlyn in his arms.

"It's Murphy. Get back to headquarters ASAP. You'd better bring the woman with you."

Chapter Twelve

Kaitlyn had wanted to get inside Big Sky Bounty Hunters headquarters for years, but she'd never even driven by the building because, until tonight, she'd never known the exact location. The place was very remote, and from the outside, looked indistinguishable from other log-cabin-style houses in the region.

Inside, the rustic charm had carried over, but Kaitlyn gave the decor only a cursory glance because guessing what was behind all those closed doors had her curiosity buzzing.

Aidan led her into a kind of great room furnished with leather furniture, big-screen TV, dart board and a pool table before disappearing inside one of those closed rooms.

Kaitlyn wandered about the room, growing more restless by the moment. If Aidan didn't return soon, she just might have to go exploring.

Rolling a billiard ball back and forth on the table, Kaitlyn glanced up to find someone watching her from the doorway. She straightened. "Hello, there."

The tiny girl looked to be around four, and she was dressed for bed in a pink-flowered nightgown with a ruffled hem. A more incongruent persona Kaitlyn could not have imagined seeing in the headquarters of a world-renowned bounty-hunting firm.

The little girl rubbed her dark eyes. "I'm not allowed to talk to strangers," she announced solemnly.

"That's a good rule," Kaitlyn said.

"Olivia!" someone called from the hallway. A moment later, a gorgeous brunette with a killer body appeared in the doorway. "There you are," she said a trifle impatiently. "What are you doing out of bed? *Again.*"

"Thirsty, Mama."

"Thirsty! Livvy, there's a glass of water by the bed. I brought it to you myself not ten minutes ago." The woman glanced up and rolled her eyes. "Hello. You must be Kaitlyn. Aidan's friend. I'm Mia Murphy."

The two women shook hands and then Mia said proudly, "This is my daughter, Olivia."

Kaitlyn bent. "Hello, Olivia. What a beautiful name. I'm Kaitlyn."

Olivia Murphy reached out and ran her fingers through Kaitlyn's hair, her eyes widening in wonder. "Look, Mama! It's fairy-princess hair!"

"Why…thank you. I think," Kaitlyn murmured.

Mia laughed. "She doesn't see too many blondes around this place. Not as fair as you anyway. And, yes, fairy-princess hair is high praise, indeed."

"Well, then I'm flattered." Kaitlyn smiled at the little girl.

"Okay," Mia said sternly. "You met the nice lady, now it's time to go back to bed. Again. No getting up this time, okay? I'd be in bed myself if your father didn't need my help."

"I want a story," the little girl declared stubbornly.

"It's too late for another story, and besides, mommy has to go help Daddy for a little while."

"Why can't Daddy come read me a story?"

"Because he's called a very important meeting, and he wants me there with him. Now, come on. Off you go."

Olivia turned her attention to Kaitlyn. "Do you have to work?" she asked slyly.

"Olivia Murphy, have you no shame!" Mia shook her head. "She's not very subtle, is she? She gets that from her father."

Kaitlyn laughed. "Well, as it happens, I don't have to work right now, and I'd love to read you a story."

"You don't have to do that," Mia protested.

"No, I'd like to. That is, if it's okay with you?" She probably should have asked for permission first, Kaitlyn realized, especially considering the late hour. She wasn't all that familiar with protocol when it came to kids and their parents.

Before her mother could protest further, Olivia hurried over and slipped her hand in Kaitlyn's.

"Well, I guess that's settled," Mia said with a sigh. "Do *not* let her con you into two stories. It's after midnight, for goodness' sake. Do you want to turn into a pumpkin?" She shook her finger at Olivia.

The little girl giggled and clutched Kaitlyn's hand.

"One story and then we're done. Scout's honor." Kaitlyn glanced down and winked at Olivia.

The little girl beamed. "Come on." She tugged on Kaitlyn's arm.

"First door on the right at the top of the stairs," Mia called after them.

And then she said something under her breath that sounded very much like "Sucker!"

AIDAN WATCHED as Mia Murphy entered the room and took a seat at the conference table beside her husband. Joseph Brown, Owen Cook, and Anthony Lombardi were also present, but the other bounty hunters were either home asleep or out in the field on assignment.

Murphy turned and said something to his wife in a low voice, and Aidan heard Mia respond, "She's finally in bed, but only after she coerced Aidan's friend into reading her another story."

"Kaitlyn?" Aidan asked in surprise.

Mia turned. "Yes. She's upstairs right now with Olivia."

Aidan and Murphy simultaneously swiveled to the bank of monitors on one side of the room. With the push of a button, Murphy could activate various security cameras that were located in every room of the building. He turned on the camera in his daughter's room now, and Olivia and Kaitlyn appeared on the screen.

Kaitlyn was sitting on the edge of the bed, and though the audio was off, Aidan could see that the two of them were laughing and talking and seemingly getting on as if they'd known each other forever.

He'd never seen Kaitlyn like that before, and for the longest moment, Aidan couldn't tear himself away from the screen. When he finally did, he caught Mia's eye and she smiled knowingly.

Satisfied that his daughter was safe and in good hands, Murphy, too, turned from the monitors. "You're probably wondering why I called you back out here at such a late hour, but there've been some new developments in the situation that I thought you all should know about. I'll brief everyone else on a need-to-know basis."

"New developments regarding Fowler?" Joseph Brown asked, from the end of the table. He was scowling as usual, but Aidan knew the late hour had very little to do with his sour disposition. According to some of the other guys, Brown had been in a bad mood ever since his wife left him three years ago. But the man's personal life wasn't any of Aidan's business. He had his own problems.

"Possibly," Murphy said. "It involves the body that Campbell and Clark discovered yesterday near Devil's Canyon. Whether Fowler and his goons were responsible is yet to be determined. But thanks to Kaitlyn Wilson, we now have a lead on the guy's identity. Does the name Wilhelm Schroeder mean anything to any of you?"

"He's the German ambassador to the U.N.," Owen Cook, their computer expert, responded. "I've been tracking this Lukin-burg thing even before Petrov's speech, and for months Wilhelm Schroeder has been one of the staunchest opponents of military intervention. After Petrov's appearance before the U.N., however, he did an about-face and now says he'll vote in favor of the resolution."

"Wait a minute," Aidan said in confusion. "You're not saying the John Doe we found is Wilhelm Schroeder, are you? What would a U.N. ambassador be doing in Montana?"

"Yeah, that's a good question," Cook agreed. "But I've been picking up some chatter online for a while now about a secret Security Council vote."

"Why secret?" Lombardi asked.

"Because the feds are afraid of a terrorist attack on the day of the vote," Murphy said. "Evidently, they perceive the threat as real and specific enough to raise the alert to the highest level and move the Security Council out of the U.N. building."

"But why Montana?" Aidan persisted.

"Our illustrious governor has some pretty important connections inside the Beltway,"

Murphy said. "If he could successfully lobby to have the vote take place here, then I'm sure he'd consider it a major feather in his cap. But that aside, a Montana retreat is not without precedence. There's a place in the Rockies that was used as far back as World War II by Churchill and Roosevelt and there was even some talk of bringing the president here after the nine-eleven attack instead of taking him to NORAD. I've never seen the place, but I've heard it's situated so that anyone approaching by ground or air can be spotted for miles. And once inside, the place is virtually impenetrable."

"And you think Schroeder was on his way to this retreat when he was killed," Aidan said. "What about his staff, bodyguards, driver? Someone like that usually has dozens of people traveling with him."

"Not if he was trying to keep the media in the dark about the secret vote. Traveling with a large entourage would have looked pretty suspicious," Murphy said. "And according to my contact at the FBI, Schroeder was known for dismissing his staff and bodyguards in order to keep his trysts with married women out of the public eye. Supposedly, he's been with his latest mistress for the past few days, but she came forward a day or two ago and said that she hadn't seen him in over a week. That's when the FBI was called in."

"Okay," Brown said, still with that dark scowl. "So what does all this mean? We have the possibility of a secret U.N. Security Council vote taking place in a secret location. An ambassador on his way to said location is murdered and his body mutilated to keep it from being identified. I'd say security for that little meeting has been badly compromised."

"No meeting, no vote, no war." Lombardi succinctly summed it all up.

"Exactly," Murphy said. "And I think it's pretty obvious who would have the most to gain from that."

"What I don't understand is how Boone Fowler figures into this," Aidan said. "Why would he care about a U.N. Security Council vote? He's a home-grown terrorist with his own agenda. He's never been interested in international politics."

"We don't know that he is involved," Murphy said. "But regardless, our mission hasn't changed. Fowler is still our target. As far as I'm concerned, the feds can deal with the rest of this mess. There is one thing, though, that is our problem." Murphy's eyes met Aidan's. "My contact was very interested in knowing where I came across the information about John Doe's German. I managed to keep Kaitlyn Wilson's name out of the conversation, but sooner or later, they're going to put it together, and they'll want to talk to her. Which might not be a bad thing, considering they could put her in protective custody until this whole thing blows over."

"I don't think so," Aidan said. "I agree with Brown. Schroeder's murder proves that the security around this secret vote has been badly compromised. If someone could get to him, what would keep them from getting to Kaitlyn in protective custody? She'd be a sitting duck."

Murphy shrugged. "What's the alternative? Stash her somewhere for the time being?"

"She'd never go for that," Aidan said. "Right now, the FBI knows everything she knows. She hasn't remembered anything else. If and when she does, we'll contact the feds, but for now, until we know exactly what we're dealing with, she's safer with me than in their custody."

"He's right," Mia said. She placed her hand on her husband's arm.

Murphy frowned. "Two days ago, we were still wondering if this woman had connections to Boone Fowler. Now she's upstairs reading a bedtime story to my daughter."

"She's not connected to Fowler," Aidan said. "I'd stake my life on it."

Murphy's expression turned grim. "You just may have to."

ON THE WAY BACK to town that night, Aidan filled Kaitlyn in on the details of the meeting. "A lot of what I've just told you is speculation," he said. "And it has to be off-the-record."

"I understand." She lifted a hand to tug back her hair. "But my head is spinning here, Aidan. The body you found near Devil's Canyon was the German ambassador to the U.N. He was on his way to a secret meeting to cast a secret vote that would allow coalition forces to invade Lukinburg. Someone killed him to keep him from casting his vote. This doesn't sound like something that would happen in Montana. It sounds like something that would happen in a Tom Clancy novel."

"We're not dealing with fiction here, Kaitlyn. You didn't just witness a murder. You witnessed an execution that could have international political ramifications."

"Don't think I haven't thought of that," Kaitlyn said uneasily. "But why are you guys involved in all this? You're bounty hunters. International intrigue is hardly in your job description, is it?"

"We're only involved to the extent that it's somehow connected to Boone Fowler. He remains our target."

"And if he's not involved? That would void our little agreement, wouldn't it, Aidan? You'd no longer need to use me to draw him out."

"Whether he's involved or not doesn't change the fact that your life is in danger.

Unless you want to take your chances in federal custody, you're stuck with me."

Kaitlyn could think of worse things. She studied his profile for a moment. He kept checking his rearview mirror until she turned to stare out the back glass. "What is it?"

"A car has been trailing us for the past several miles."

Kaitlyn could barely pick out the lights in the distance. "They may not be following us," she said. "This is a public road."

"Yeah, but it's also remote and nearly one o'clock in the morning."

Kaitlyn glanced out the back glass again, then turned to watch the road. In spite of the fact that they might have a tail, Kaitlyn wished Aidan would slow down. He was traveling fast on a two-lane highway that zigzagged down the mountain. Keeping one eye on the rearview mirror, he took the hairpin turns at a breathtaking speed.

They were coming upon another curve. Kaitlyn clutched the edge of her seat as they seemed to slide into the turn on two wheels. Aidan again glanced in the rearview mirror, but Kaitlyn was staring straight ahead. She was the first to see the boulder that had rolled onto the road, directly into their path.

"Aidan, watch out!"

He saw the boulder a split second after she did. Pumping the brakes, he cut the wheel hard to avoid impact, but the moment they hit the loose gravel on the shoulder of the road, the vehicle went into a spin. When Aidan finally had the wheel under control, they were heading straight for the embankment.

"Hold on!" he yelled.

They went over the edge, and for what seemed an eternity, the Jeep bounded over rocks and underbrush until it finally bottomed out on a boulder and jerked to a stop.

Kaitlyn's heart was pounding so hard she could hardly breathe, but she didn't think she was seriously hurt. Just a little jarred.

"Are you all right?" Aidan asked worriedly.

"I think so." Other than feeling as if her teeth might have been rattled loose, she was fine.

"We've got to get out of here. I'm not so sure that boulder rolled down the mountain on its own."

Kaitlyn whipped her head around. "What do you mean? It was a trap?"

"Maybe." Aidan reached across her and opened the glove box. After taking out a gun, he slid in a clip and released the safety. "Do you know how to use this?"

She nodded. "I can manage."

No sooner had she spoken, than the back glass shattered into a million pieces. Kaitlyn screamed.

"Get down!" Aidan shouted.

Flinging open the door, he all but dragged Kaitlyn out behind him. Then he opened fire as they dove for cover behind several boulders that were at the base of the embankment.

"Keep them honest," Aidan said as he snatched his cell phone from his pocket and lifted it to his ear. "But don't waste bullets. Once we're out of ammo, we're in big trouble."

"Who are you calling?"

"Someone I can trust." He dialed the number, then said, "It's Campbell." Quickly he described the situation and the location. "We need backup ASAP."

A new round of shots rang out, and Kaitlyn returned the fire. "How long before help gets here?"

"Hopefully, soon."

Aidan fired back, too, but it was only a matter of minutes before they'd both be out of ammo.

"I've only got a couple of shots left," she said. "What happens when we run out?"

"We'll have to make a run for it," Aidan told her.

Run where? Kaitlyn wanted to know, but just then she heard the distant *whop-whop* of a chopper, and in another few moments, she saw the lights.

The helicopter was flying low and fast, and when it crossed the highway, a spotlight came on, illuminating wide swatches of the dark landscape.

The jump door was open and two men with automatic weapons were crouched in the opening. The moment the chopper set down, they jumped out and began to spray the area with bullets.

Aidan grabbed Kaitlyn's hand. "Come on!"

They ran for the chopper and Aidan helped

Kaitlyn inside. Then one of the men threw him a weapon, and they continued to fire as the chopper began to lift off.

"Wait a minute!" Kaitlyn cried. "They're not on board!"

The pilot tossed her a headset and Kaitlyn put it on as she climbed into the front with him.

"Buckle up," he said with a grin. "You're in for one hell of a ride."

POWELL CIRCLED the area with the spotlight as Aidan and the others beat the bushes on the ground, but after nearly forty-five minutes of searching, they had to finally admit that the gunmen had managed to get away, which meant whoever had set up the attack obviously knew the terrain.

As soon as Murphy sent reinforcements, Powell flew Aidan and Kaitlyn to a safe house in the mountains where they'd be able to get a few hours of rest without having to worry about an ambush.

But as Kaitlyn watched the helicopter lift off, lights twinkling in the night sky, she wondered if she would ever be able to sleep again.

Aidan had grabbed a blanket from the chopper as they disembarked, and now he draped it around her shoulders as they trudged from the clearing where Powell had landed to a small A-frame cabin that seemed to be perched on the edge of a cliff.

Kaitlyn stood on the porch shivering as Aidan unlocked the door. "Who owns this place?"

"Some of my buddies and I bought it a few years ago," he said. "We come up here to snowboard in the winter and rock climb in the summer."

Climbing rocks sounded dangerous to Kaitlyn. And like a lot of work.

Aidan opened the door and stepped in first to turn on the lights.

"I'm surprised you have electricity," Kaitlyn murmured.

"We're not that rustic," Aidan said with a grin. "Make yourself at home. I'll turn on the heat and get a fire going. We'll get this place warmed up in no time."

While he busied himself with the fire,

Kaitlyn walked slowly around the room. The place was small and furnished for comfort, not style, with mismatched overstuffed furniture and a few scattered rugs to warm up the wood floor.

Snowshoes hung on the walls, along with a few fishing rods and a framed photograph that Kaitlyn walked over to take a closer look at. It was an aerial view of a group of rock climbers scaling what appeared to be a vertical wall that seemed to rise endlessly toward the sky. It gave Kaitlyn a breathless sensation, just staring at the photo.

"Are you in this picture?" she asked Aidan.

He glanced up. "Yeah."

"Who are the other guys?"

"Some of the rescue climbers I worked with in Colorado after I left Special Ops."

"Rescue climbers? Does that mean you rescued other climbers when they got into trouble?"

"Among other things."

Kaitlyn reexamined the photograph. "And then for fun you climbed more rocks, right? You know what I like to do for fun? I rent movies and make popcorn."

Aidan smiled. "I like that, too."

He returned to the fire and Kaitlyn crossed the room to stare at the view. The wall of windows looked out on the edge of the cliff, but at night, there was nothing to see but blackness below and a sky filled with stars above. It almost gave the sensation of being suspended on the edge of the universe.

"Come over by the fire," Aidan said. "We'll get you warmed up in no time."

She turned to join him. Placing her trembling hands over the fire, she said, "You wouldn't happen to have something to drink up here, would you? Something stronger than coffee or hot chocolate, I mean."

"We've probably got something stashed around here somewhere. Just keep warming yourself. I'll be right back."

But instead, Kaitlyn followed him into the small kitchen and watched as he opened a cupboard. "How about a shot of whiskey?" he said, taking down a bottle and two glasses.

"Sounds good to me."

He stood at a small island in the center of the kitchen and poured the drinks. Before he could propose a toast, though, Kaitlyn lifted her glass and downed the contents. She wasn't used to anything stronger than wine or beer, but the fiery liquid was just what she needed. She placed her glass on the counter and Aidan poured her another.

"You're not trying to get me drunk, are you?" She didn't really care if he was or not. At the moment, getting drunk sounded like an excellent idea.

"This was your idea," he reminded her. He finished his own drink and watched as she downed her second.

Kaitlyn licked her numb lips. "How come you're so calm about all this? Your hands are as steady as a rock. Look at mine." She held them out and showed him how badly they were still trembling.

"It's not the first time I've been shot at," he said.

She kept forgetting about his past. "A Special Forces soldier, a rescue climber, and now a bounty hunter."

She licked her lips again. "You know what I think you are? You're one of those adrenaline junkies."

He leaned his elbows on the counter as

he regarded her with a bemused look. "Is that so?"

"You get off on danger. Like those guys who jump out of airplanes in the troposphere."

"Nothing like free-falling from the edge of space," he said.

"You've done that, too?" Kaitlyn shuddered as she poured herself another drink. "There's a guy in Eagle Falls that used to be in Special Forces. I interviewed him once. He's a graduate of the Military Freefall Jumpmaster School in Yuma, Arizona. He runs a skydiving company that includes tandem freefall. For a few hundred bucks, he'll take you up to fifty thousand feet, strap you to him, and jump out of the plane. Not exactly my idea of a great time."

Aidan feigned shock. "What, you didn't do it? What kind of reporter are you?"

She propped her elbows on the counter and shrugged. "The cowardly kind," she freely admitted.

"Seriously, you should try it sometime. There's nothing like it."

She groaned. "Please don't tell me it's better than sex. That's such a cliché."

"Better than sex? Hmm." He seemed to consider it for a moment. "I'd have to say that all depends."

On what? Kaitlyn wanted to ask him, but the look he gave her pretty much said it all.

The look that implied that she could jump out of a hundred airplanes and the thrills wouldn't equate to spending one single night with him.

That look.

Slowly, she put down her glass.

Chapter Thirteen

Their gazes clung for the longest moment, and then bending across the counter, Aidan kissed her. Maybe that was all he meant it to be. A simple kiss. Some sort of comfort or warmth she could cling to in order to assuage her fears.

But the moment his lips touched hers, something came unleashed inside Kaitlyn and, sliding her fingers into his hair, she pulled him even closer, grinding her mouth against his as their tongues mated desperately.

Somehow Aidan ended up on the same side of the counter as she, and grabbing her around the waist, he lifted her up to the smooth surface, kissing her again as his fingers deftly unfastened her blouse and then slid it down her arms. She wasn't quite as accomplished in the undressing department, so she ended up ripping apart his shirt, sending the buttons flying in every direction.

Aidan didn't seem to mind. In fact, her actions caused his eyes to darken with something that made Kaitlyn tremble, though not with fear. He grabbed her and kissed her again, hard and fast and desperate, and then trailed his lips down her throat, teasing her breasts through her lacy bra.

Kaitlyn leaned back on her hands, her heart beating so hard she could hear it in her ears as Aidan's fingers slid inside the waistband of her jeans to unsnap them.

He didn't remove them, though, until they were in the bedroom. Kaitlyn lay on top of the covers as he tugged off her jeans, and then rising to her knees, she skimmed her lips along his washboard abs as her fingers found his zipper.

A second later, they were both naked, and as Kaitlyn watched Aidan lower himself over her, she began to tremble even harder. Part of it was still the aftermath of danger. She knew that. But mostly it was the thought of what they were about to do.

There was nothing gentle about the way they came together, but Kaitlyn didn't want gentle. It hadn't been a gentle night. It had been dark and dangerous, even savage, and a tender coupling wasn't something either of them could have managed at the moment.

What they needed was an immediate release from all of the adrenaline still rushing through their veins, and as Aidan thrust inside her, Kaitlyn's was almost instant. She couldn't stop it. It burst over her in wave after wave of sensation, more powerful than any she had ever experienced before, and prolonged, it seemed, by the intensity of Aidan's shuddering response.

He held her until both their shudders subsided, then he rolled over and lay on his back next to her. Hearts still pounding, they lay side by side in complete silence. After a moment, Aidan reached down, took her hand and squeezed it.

It was the only communication Kaitlyn needed.

AIDAN HADN'T WANTED their first time to be that way. He'd wanted to make love to Kaitlyn slowly, savoring every inch of her beautiful body, but the moment he'd touched her, he hadn't been able to control himself.

Later, when they went in to shower, he told himself it would be different this time. But there she stood, all wet and naked, her eyes telling him that she didn't need slow and deliberate, she wanted it fast and desperate again. And then she showed him she meant business, first with her hands and then with her mouth.

He lifted her in his arms and kissed her roughly as he pressed her back against the tile wall, thrusting inside her until they both shuddered to another mind-blowing climax.

Afterward, they climbed into bed and slept for a while, and it wasn't until they awakened sometime in the afternoon that Aidan was finally able to make love to her the way he'd always intended.

He started with her feet, massaging first one then the other between the palms of his hands until her muscles turned to Jell-O and she sighed with pleasure. Then he slid his hands up her legs, teasing them open as he bent to kiss the insides of her thighs. With a soft groan, she opened even more for him, and he took his time with her, pulling away when he sensed she was getting a little too frantic, giving her a moment to calm before starting the slow buildup all over again.

He explored every inch of her with his hands and his lips and his tongue. Finally she threaded her fingers in his hair and tugged him up to her, kissing him so deeply that Aidan's control began to waver. And when her hand slipped around him, guiding him to her, he couldn't have stopped at that moment if his life depended on it.

He rolled them over, and Kaitlyn lowered herself over him, moving so slowly and deliberately that Aidan realized it was he who had been seduced.

LATE-AFTERNOON SUNLIGHT streamed in from the window and slanted across Kaitlyn's face as she slowly opened her eyes. It took her a moment to remember where she was, and then, as it all came back to her, she turned over so that she could watch Aidan sleep. But he was already awake, lying on his back and staring at the ceiling.

She rolled onto her stomach and, wrapping an arm around his lean waist, she placed her chin on his shoulder. "Hey," she said softly.

"Hey."

"You look so serious," she said with a frown. "What are you thinking about?"

"Not really thinking about anything. Just letting my mind wander," he said with a shrug.

"Some day, huh?"

"Yeah." He kissed her hair. "Some day."

"Can I ask you something, Aidan?"

His lips were still in her hair. "What is it?"

"What made you join the service? Was your father a military man?"

"Why would you think that?"

She shrugged. "Military service is sometimes a family tradition, right?"

"In some families, I guess. But my father is a corporate attorney in Los Angeles."

"Really?" Kaitlyn didn't know why that revelation surprised her, but it did. "Then what made you decide to join up?"

"I didn't have much of a choice." For a moment, Kaitlyn thought he wouldn't elaborate, but then he shrugged as he scowled at the ceiling. "I was the kind of kid who got into one scrape after another. Alcohol, drugs, you name it. I had a fast car, money to burn, and enough family connections to keep me out of trouble. It's amazing what you can get by with when you flash an ID with a Beverly Hills address on it." His words were flip, but there was something dark in his voice.

It was shame, Kaitlyn realized. A shame so deep that he couldn't quite bring himself to look at her.

What had he done? What could possibly be so bad that he hadn't been able to forgive himself all these years later? she wondered

"I won't bore you with the details," he said, as if anticipating her next question.

"Then give me the condensed version," Kaitlyn urged softly. She turned to him. "I'm not trying to pry, Aidan. I just want to know something about you."

"You already know something about me."

"Yes, let's see. You've been a soldier, a rescue ranger and a bounty hunter. You climb rocks and like to jump out of airplanes for fun. But now I'd like to hear about your childhood."

"I wasn't a child when I joined the service, Kaitlyn. I was a grown man on my way to becoming a convicted felon."

She drew back in shock. "What? What did you do?"

"When I was nineteen, some of my friends and I decided to boost a car. We took it for a joy ride, wrapped it around a light pole, and two of my buddies died in the crash, another in the hospital two weeks later."

"Oh, my God," Kaitlyn whispered.

"Yeah, I was lucky, although I didn't think so at the time. Going to those funerals and facing those families…" He broke off, and Kaitlyn knew that the shame and guilt from that tragedy had probably shaped his entire life. Was that why he felt such a need to rescue people? Was he still trying to making amends?

"I wasn't driving or I could have been charged with vehicular homicide," he said. "As it was, I was looking at some pretty stiff charges, but my father had some pull with the judge who heard my case. He had the guy give me an ultimatum. I could either serve time in San Quentin or serve my country. I enlisted the next day."

"So you went from Beverly Hills to boot camp," Kaitlyn said. "Talk about culture shock."

He gave a little laugh. "Yeah, it was a real eye-opener. But it was also the best thing that ever happened to me. Gave me discipline, focus, a sense of self-worth." He shrugged. "Old story. You've heard it a million times."

"Okay, that explains why you joined up. Now tell me why you left."

"It was time to move on. You can understand that, can't you?"

"Sure. But was it really that simple?"

"What do you mean?"

Kaitlyn rolled over on her back and stared at the ceiling. "Last night, right before Murphy called, when we were on the floor…you know…" She smiled. "I reached for your wallet, remember? I saw a picture of a woman inside."

He turned to stare at her.

"I wasn't snooping. It just opened up to that picture." Kaitlyn hesitated. "Who is she, Aidan?"

He refocused his attention on the ceiling. "Her name was Elena Sanchez."

"Was?"

"She's dead."

Kaitlyn exhaled slowly. "I'm sorry. Was she…someone close to you?" Of course, she was. Why else would he carry around her picture?

"We were engaged for a while."

She turned to prop herself on her elbow as she stared at him. "Aidan, I'm so sorry. I had no idea. If you don't want to talk about her, I understand."

But she wanted him to talk about Elena Sanchez, Kaitlyn realized. She wanted him to say that he'd known her a long time ago. That he was over her. She was nothing but a memory to him now.

"I met her five years ago," he finally said. "It was right before Colonel Murphy resigned his commission and our unit broke up. Elena and her family were from Colombia. Her father worked for one of the drug cartels, but he was also a CIA informant. When his cover was compromised, we were sent in to get him and his family out."

"Did you?"

"Yes. We brought them back to the States and Elena and I began seeing each other."

"You fell in love," Kaitlyn said.

"We were together for two years, and then it was over."

Kaitlyn looked at him in surprise. "What happened?"

"I was away a lot. She was lonely." He paused. "She'd been a medical student at the National Academy of Medicine in Bogotá. She'd had a brilliant future ahead of her, and then suddenly her whole life was ripped apart. She had a hard time adjusting and I tried to compensate. But I finally realized that the engagement was a mistake for both of us because I was never going to be able to give her back what she'd lost. And she was always going to resent me for that."

"Were you still in love with her?"

"I don't know. The relationship was complicated. I felt a lot of things for her...but love? I'm not so sure anymore."

What *had* he felt for Elena? Kaitlyn wondered. Had he felt protective of her? Had he felt responsible for her because he'd saved her?

Those same emotions he seemed to now have projected onto Kaitlyn.

The notion made her more than a little uncomfortable.

"Just over a year ago, I found out she'd gone back to Colombia to find her brother. He'd joined a group of rebel insurgents somewhere in the mountains, and Elena had heard from a friend that he'd been badly wounded. She went to find him."

"And you went to find her," Kaitlyn said. "Did you?"

"Yes, finally. Her brother had died, and Elena had had to go into hiding. I found her in a remote village in the Andes. She was in bad shape, emotionally and physically, and it was risky to move her, but more dangerous to leave her. I'd arranged for a helicopter to pick us up, but I had to get her to the rendezvous point."

He took a deep breath and Kaitlyn couldn't help noticing how his hands were trembling ever so slightly. Whatever he was about to tell her, she sensed it wasn't going to be easy.

"We were crossing a rope bridge over a ravine one night. She was terrified of heights, and she slipped. I caught her and I could have pulled her to safety, but she panicked and started to struggle. I tried to calm her, but she was too scared. And every time I tried to pull her up, she became even more frantic. I could feel her slipping away from me, and there wasn't a damn thing I could do about it. She fell, begging me not to let her die."

Kaitlyn closed her eyes and shuddered. "I'm sorry," she whispered. It sounded lame, but what else was there to say?

"Guilt is such a funny thing." She put out a tentative hand to touch his arm, then drew it back. He seemed so remote at the moment. So lost in his own pain that Kaitlyn wasn't sure he'd welcome her comfort. "You can see it so clearly when someone else is beating themselves up needlessly, but when it comes to your own guilt—" she shrugged "—reason doesn't seem to matter. You can tell yourself a million times that it wasn't your fault. She was a grown woman. It was her decision to go back to Colombia and put herself in that kind of danger. You did everything you could to save her, but…"

"It wasn't enough."

"It wasn't enough." Kaitlyn stared at the ceiling for a moment. "I can't tell you how many times I've told myself that what happened to Jenny wasn't my fault. I didn't make her join the MMFAFA. She was a grown woman. She made that decision on her own. But when she came to me for help, what did I do? I sent her back in."

Aidan turned to face her. "That was her decision, too. She could have refused."

"But she didn't. And I've had to live with the consequences. So...I guess what I'm saying is that I know about guilt, Aidan. It doesn't matter what anyone says, or how much you try to convince yourself otherwise, until you're ready to accept the fact that there wasn't anything more you could have done to save Elena, you'll have this burden. You might never get over it. But you will eventually get past it."

She saw him smile in the fading light. "Not only brave, but wise. You really are quite a woman, you know that?"

Kaitlyn didn't feel so brave or so wise at the moment. What she felt was a bit foolish.

She cared about Aidan. She cared about him a lot. If she wasn't careful, she could easily fall in love with him, and what a mistake that would be. Because whether he wanted to admit it or not, what he felt for her had *rebound* written all over it.

AFTER THAT CONVERSATION, Kaitlyn began to put the brakes on their relationship. She tried to do it subtly, but she had a feeling Aidan knew exactly what she was doing.

So be it. She had to protect herself because the longer they stayed together, the harder it would be for her to leave him. And she would have to leave him eventually. For one thing, she had a career to think of. And for another…the man was still nursing some very deep and complex feelings for another woman. A *dead* woman. And there was no way Kaitlyn wanted to compete with that.

And why should she have to? She had a full life without Aidan, and she needed to get back to that life and forget about losing herself in his arms…just one last time.

They stayed at the cabin until Monday

morning, and then Kaitlyn told him that she wanted to return to Ponderosa.

"I can't hide out forever," she'd insisted. "I have a job. Deadlines. Responsibilities. I'd have to go back before the weekend anyway because I'm covering the governor's ball at the Denning mansion on Saturday night. After that, it's the governor's whistle-stop tour through the state."

Aidan frowned. "Whistle-stop tour? When did that come about?"

"It's been planned for a while. The train is scheduled to leave sometime after the ball, and Eden has asked me to ride along in the press car. I can't back out now. I owe her. And then, of course, the election is coming up...."

"Okay, I get your point," Aidan had said a bit testily, but he'd called Powell anyway to come pick them up.

By the time they got back to Kaitlyn's apartment, everything had changed between them. Before, Kaitlyn's intense attraction to Aidan had been the elephant in the room that kept her on edge, but now it was the ghost of Elena Sanchez that had become the intruder.

That night, Kaitlyn said good-night to Aidan, went into her bedroom, closed the door and didn't come out again until the following morning. He didn't question her decision. He didn't say a word about the wall she'd erected between them, but his silent acquiescence told Kaitlyn everything she needed to know, and then some.

"IF I CAN'T TRUST YOU to carry out one simple task, how can I have any faith that you'll be able to pull off the next phase of the operation?"

Boone Fowler shrugged. "What choice do you have?"

"We always have choices, my friend." The man smiled thinly. "You said you would take care of Kaitlyn Wilson, and yet my sources tell me that she's returned to her apartment in Ponderosa, apparently without so much as a scratch. How is that possible?"

"I'll tell you how it's possible." Fowler rose slowly, his hand tightening around the knife he'd been holding under the table. Now he lifted it to the light to make sure his companion saw the gleam of the blade. "She has a bodyguard…one of Cameron Murphy's men. And she has the full protection of Murphy's outfit behind her. I say we take them out first."

"And have the whole operation explode in our faces? I don't think so. You had your chance, Fowler. Now it's my turn."

"What are you going to do?"

"What I should have done from the first. Take care of the problem myself."

The man never got his hands dirty. He had something else up his sleeve. "You're going to kill her yourself," Fowler scoffed. "That I'd like to see."

"Well, then, stick around, my friend. The arrangements have already been made. After Saturday night, Kaitlyn Wilson will be nothing more than a bad memory."

Fowler almost smiled at that. The pompous fool had no idea that the same fate he'd planned for Kaitlyn Wilson…also awaited him.

Chapter Fourteen

Saturday, 2000 hours

"Cook has picked up some interesting chatter from the Internet," Murphy told them late Saturday afternoon as they assembled around the conference table in the war room. "And my FBI contact has reluctantly confirmed that the terror threat level has been raised, not just in Washington but here in Montana as well."

"Is this the result of the hit on the German ambassador?" someone asked him.

"Why don't you explain what you've been hearing?" Murphy told Cook.

Owen nodded. "I've been monitoring a lot of the same chat rooms and bulletin boards that the feds keep an eye on, from what I've been able to tell, it seems that the hit on the ambassador was nothing more than a decoy. Something bigger is in the works."

"Like what?"

"I don't know for sure," Cook said. "But today's date keeps popping up, and the only thing I can come up with is the governor's ball. I haven't come across anything concrete, but with Petrov in attendance, it makes sense it could be a target."

Aidan's heart thudded against his chest. "Are you talking about an assassination attempt or something more than that?" Because Kaitlyn was going to be at the ball… she was probably already there by now.

His fingers itched to grab his cell phone and call her, but he needed to hear Cook out first. He had to know exactly what he was dealing with here.

"I'm talking about a bomb," Cook said bluntly.

Aidan swore.

"We think that's why they needed Fowler," Murphy said. "We couldn't figure out why Boone Fowler would get involved in an international plot, but this could be our answer. Who better to blow up a building filled with innocent people than an old pro like Fowler?"

Aidan sat forward, the adrenaline rushing through his veins making him almost light-headed. "We have to get that building evacuated immediately."

Murphy frowned. "Unfortunately, that's easier said than done."

"There must be some way. Call your FBI contact." Aidan jumped to his feet. "For God's sakes, we can't just sit here. We have to get those people out of there."

Murphy shook his head. "It's too late. The place is packed, and they're not going to evacuate because of some conjecture on our part. The feds have agreed to increase security, but that's it. The rest is up to us. I'm sending a couple of you inside, and then I want the rest of you surrounding that building."

"I'm going in," Aidan said.

Murphy's first instinct was to deny him. Aidan could see it in his eyes. He could almost hear the colonel gearing up for his conflict-of-interest speech, but Aidan wasn't having it. Not this time. Not with Kaitlyn's life on the line.

How and when she'd become so important to him didn't seem to matter at the moment. Aidan would ponder those questions later, along with all the reasons why a long-term relationship wasn't in the cards for them.

Right now, though, nothing mattered but getting to her as quickly as possible.

He and Murphy stared at each other for a moment, then Murphy finally nodded. "All right. You and Brown will work from the inside. The rest of you, keep your eyes peeled. If Fowler slips through our net, we could have another tragedy on our hands."

And Kaitlyn would be right smack in the middle of it.

EDEN COULDN'T HAVE GOTTEN better weather for the governor's ball if she'd placed a special order for it, Kaitlyn decided as she stepped out of the car and presented her ID and invitation to the security detail in charge of scrutinizing the guests. The night was cool and clear, with only a slight nip of fall in the air and not the slightest hint of the rain that had been forecasted all week.

Slipping her ID into her bag, Kaitlyn's excitement mounted as she headed up the steps of the Denning mansion. Kaitlyn had spent the first fourteen years of her life in Washington, D.C., with a newsman father, so she wasn't unaccustomed to lavish political events such as this. But meeting a real-life prince…that didn't happen to a girl every day.

Kaitlyn was asked to show her ID again at the door, and then finally she was inside. She'd never been to the Denning mansion before although she'd seen lots of pictures. The photographs hadn't done the place justice, though. It was all white marble, graceful columns and gilded ceilings—a magnificent, elegant home that belonged somewhere in the south of France, not plopped down on the outskirts of Helena, Montana.

Tonight, with the swirling ball gowns and glittering masks, it seemed even more old-world and aristocratic.

Kaitlyn felt a bit ridiculous holding up her own mask to hide her identity, but everyone else had joined in the spirit of the evening, and when in Rome…

As she made her way through the crowd,

she realized the evening already looked to be a success. The place was packed. Eden had to be ecstatic about the turnout. And everyone seemed to be having such a marvelous time. It was very lavish and festive, with the women laughing and flirting behind elaborate disguises and the men, all handsome and mysterious, in their tuxes and plain black masks.

Kaitlyn had only been inside for a few minutes when the governor took to the podium for his welcome address. In spite of Eden's connection, Kaitlyn had never formally met Peter Gilbert, although she'd attended numerous press conferences and had even managed to get in a question now and then. He was a handsome man whose charm and charisma seemed to be exceeded only by his ambition.

Kaitlyn had often wondered, but never dared asked, about Eden's relationship with Gilbert. There were rumors of an affair circulating about the state capital, and Kaitlyn had seen a look in Eden's eyes from time to time that made her wonder if those rumors were true.

She supposed it wouldn't be the first time

that a woman fell for her boss, especially one as charming and powerful as Peter Gilbert.

As eloquent as ever, he soon had the crowd laughing and nodding in agreement as he made light of the extraordinary security hoops they'd had to jump through that evening, and then he sobered. "Seriously, I do want to thank you all for coming out tonight, for all the support you've given me during my campaign, and most of all for your generous donations this evening to such a worthy cause. In times like these, we all must make sacrifices...."

In times like these...

The hair at the back of Kaitlyn's neck lifted. Where had she heard that phrase before?

Something tugged at her memory, but she couldn't quite grasp it—

"I see Gilbert is in rare form tonight," a male voice said in her ear.

Kaitlyn whirled. "Aidan?" She lifted her hand and peeked behind the mask. "It is you! What are you doing here? Why didn't you tell me you were coming? And how on earth did you get in?"

Even behind the mask, she could tell that

his expression was serious. "I need to talk to you—"

"*Shush!*" she said, as Gilbert began his introduction of Nikolai Petrov and his sister, Veronika.

The pair rose to thunderous applause and then Nikolai strode over to the microphone to say a few words.

His voice was deep and rich and he had only a slight accent. He was an accomplished speaker and as he began talking about the plight of his people in Lukinburg and the desperate need for a U.N. resolution, a hush fell over the room. There had been the usual shifting and coughing when Governor Gilbert spoke, but with Petrov, a pin could have been heard dropping. The man was electric, mesmerizing. As Kaitlyn watched him, she suddenly understood why the world had fallen so hard for Nikolai Petrov.

After his speech, the orchestra started to play again, and gradually the hall returned to normal. Aidan took Kaitlyn's arm and started to pull her away from the throng, but Eden came up just then and grabbed her other arm.

"There you are! I've been looking for you

all evening," Eden admonished. "I thought you'd stood me up!"

"I saw you earlier, but you were busy and I didn't want to bother you," Kaitlyn said. "Eden…you've outdone yourself. This event…this whole evening is extraordinary."

Eden smiled, but she seemed a bit tense as she scanned the crowd. "I never can breathe easily until these things are over." She turned back to Kaitlyn, and then nodded at Aidan. "Well, hello. It's good to see you again."

Kaitlyn thought Aidan's smile seemed a bit forced. "You, too."

Eden's focus swept over him admiringly, and Kaitlyn was surprised to feel a stab of jealousy. *He's mine,* she wanted to say, but of course, he wasn't.

So she kept her mouth shut, but she could understand why Eden couldn't seem to tear her attention away from him. The man looked absolutely gorgeous in a tux.

And she'd spent so much time fantasizing about him in a uniform, Kaitlyn thought.

Eden's grasp tightened on Kaitlyn's arm. "You didn't tell me you were bringing a date," she admonished.

"I didn't. We came separately."

"Oh…in that case…" She smiled up at Aidan. "You won't mind if I borrow Kaitlyn for a few moments? There's someone I want her to meet."

Before he could respond, Eden whisked Kaitlyn away. "Come on. It's time to meet Petrov."

And a moment later, Kaitlyn was standing in front of him. She didn't quite know the correct protocol on meeting royalty, but she wasn't the curtsying type. So she merely extended her hand and murmured, "How do you do?"

He took her hand and lifted it to his lips. Of course, he would, Kaitlyn thought. The courtly gesture suited him to a T.

"Eden tells me you're her oldest and dearest friend," he said warmly.

"Yes, we go back a long way. We went to high school together." Where was Eden? She seemed to have disappeared, and Kaitlyn couldn't help wondering if she'd beat a path back to Aidan. Had this whole thing been a ploy to separate them?

That was ridiculous. Eden had gone to great deal of trouble to engineer this meeting. The least Kaitlyn could do was show a little gratitude.

And concentrate, for God's sake. She was speaking to a prince here. And not just any old run-of-the-mill prince at that, but Nikolai Petrov!

"The friendships we make in school are often the most enduring," he said. "You're lucky to have each other."

The wistfulness in his voice made Kaitlyn realize all the things he'd left behind when he turned his back on his father's tyranny.

"Are you enjoying your stay in Montana?" she asked, hoping to prolong the conversation long enough to slip in a question or two about the situation in Lukinburg.

He clasped his hands behind his back and rocked on his heels. "It's quite a state. Rugged. Beautiful. Even a bit dangerous," he said with a gleam in his eyes. "It reminds me a little of home."

And just like that, Kaitlyn had her opening. "You must miss Lukinburg. I've never been there, of course, but my father tells me it's quite beautiful. And violent."

"Yes, the violence," he said with a sigh. His expression clouded, and for a moment,

Kaitlyn thought that he was unhappy about something she'd said, but then she realized he was looking past her.

"Would you excuse me? I see someone I must have a word with," he murmured.

And just like that, he was gone.

Kaitlyn turned and watched him make his way through the crowd. His sister, Veronika, was dancing with a man who looked vaguely familiar. He didn't have a mask on and his expression, even with a beautiful princess in his arms, was a bit dour. Try as she might, though, Kaitlyn couldn't place him.

Nikolai took his sister's arm and tried to pull her away, but she flung off his hand. The two of them exchanged a few heated words before she went back to her dance partner. And then Nikolai stomped away.

"I wonder what that was that all about," Aidan said at Kaitlyn's shoulder.

She turned. "I don't think he was too pleased to see who she was dancing with. Do you know who that guy is?"

"His name is Joseph Brown. He works with me."

"He's a bounty hunter?" Kaitlyn asked in

surprise. "What's he doing dancing with Princess Veronika? Aidan, what's going on here—"

The explosion rattled the windows in the mansion, and as Aidan grabbed Kaitlyn's arm to drag her away from glass, the place erupted in pandemonium.

"Wait here," he said. "Don't move. I'll be right back."

"Ladies and gentlemen, please remain calm," the governor said from the podium. "It's nothing but fireworks. Nothing at all to be alarmed about."

There was some nervous laughter from the crowd, but most everyone seemed too jittery to find humor in the situation. With Petrov in attendance, the threat of terrorism was on everyone's mind and the explosion had made it all seem too real.

Kaitlyn, watching from a corner, tried to calm her own racing heart while she waited for Aidan.

"I JUST GOT WORD from Murphy," Joseph Brown said a little while later. "We have to return to headquarters immediately."

"Why?" Aidan asked with a frown. "What's going on?"

"Cook has come up with some new information. He doesn't think this place is the target after all."

Aidan glanced over his shoulder at the mansion behind him. "He can't pull us out yet. What if he's wrong?"

Brown shrugged. "I'm just relaying orders. You have a problem, you take it up with the colonel."

"Good idea," Aidan said as he whipped out his cell phone. Within seconds, he heard Murphy's voice on the other end. "Colonel, what the hell is going on? Brown says you want us back at headquarters."

"This is an unsecured communication," Murphy growled. "I can't go into detail, but we got the target wrong. We're trying to nail down the new coordinates, and as soon as we have them, I need you ready to roll."

"Colonel, I can't leave. Not yet."

"Campbell, get back here now. Do you understand me? Bring Kaitlyn with you if you have to, but I want you back at headquarters ASAP. That's an order."

It was on the tip of Aidan's tongue to remind him they were no longer in the service, but instead, he severed the call and went to find Kaitlyn.

EDEN CAME UP beside Kaitlyn. "Where's Aidan?"

"He stepped outside for a few minutes. He said he'd be right back."

Eden's gaze sharpened. "Where did he go?"

"I have no idea."

"So are you ready to get out of here then?" Eden asked her.

Kaitlyn lifted a brow. "And go where?"

"The train station, remember? The whistle-stop tour? You didn't forget, did you? Because I'm counting on you."

"I didn't forget, but I can't leave until Aidan gets back. I told him I'd wait here for him."

"Call him on his cell and tell him there's been a change of plans. But don't say where you're going. That's top secret." Eden's eyes gleamed. "No one is supposed to know anything about this, so you have to keep mum until we get out of here, okay?"

"But what if he asks where I'm going? I can't lie to him."

"Then tell him it's none of his business."

"Eden! The man saved my life." More than once, Kaitlyn silently added. She might have been cool to him this past week, but there was no way she could be out-and-out rude to him. Besides…she wanted to wait for him. She wanted to go back to her apartment and pretend she'd never erected that stupid wall between them.

"Look," Eden said impatiently, "I didn't want to tell you until we were safely away from this place. I don't want anyone to overhear, but…" She leaned in closer to Kaitlyn. "Petrov is going to accompany the governor on the first leg of the trip. He's on his way to the station now. The fireworks were a diversion so that he could leave without creating a big uproar. If you want that exclusive, we'll have to leave right this minute. You don't have time to wait for Aidan. You can call him when we're in the car. Petrov will be boarding the governor's private car in fifteen minutes, and as soon as the train pulls out, he's gone for good. This is your last chance. Do you want it or not?"

Kaitlyn bit her lip. This was the opportunity of a lifetime. She didn't dare blow it. Aidan would just have to understand. Besides, his concern was for her safety. How much safer could she be? Petrov was surrounded by his own personal bodyguards as well as federal agents. No one would be able to touch her.

She turned back to Eden and nodded. "Of course, I want it. Let's go."

Eden smiled. "I had a feeling you'd say that."

She led the way through a maze of hallways so confusing that Kaitlyn was soon hopelessly lost. She doubted she could have made her way back to the ballroom if her life depended on it.

They exited the mansion through a side entrance where a car waited for them. As they slid into the back seat, Eden started to laugh.

"What's so funny?" Kaitlyn asked.

"You. Me. Look at us in our designer gowns and Manolo Blahniks."

"A far cry from the jeans and sneakers we wore in high school," Kaitlyn agreed.

"We've come a long way, baby," Eden said.

And then they both started to laugh.

AIDAN STARED at his cell phone in dismay. Kaitlyn had slipped out of the ball, and he had no idea where the hell she'd gone off to. She wouldn't say. She'd only called to reassure him that she was safe, he shouldn't worry, she'd talk to him when she got back.

Got back from where, damn it?

He snapped the cell phone shut and stuffed it in his pocket.

"Problems?" Brown asked in his usual surly manner.

"I don't know."

"Are you going back to headquarters or not?" Brown demanded. "I'm not standing around here all night waiting for you to make up your mind."

Aidan had half a mind to punch the guy right in his kisser, but instead he shrugged. "Let's get the hell out of here."

Why was he even surprised? Aidan wondered a little while later as the chopper lifted off from the pad. Ever since they'd returned from the cabin, Kaitlyn had been putting distance between them. He couldn't blame her, he supposed. Having him around all the time was bound to cramp her style, and it wasn't her fault that he'd gotten a little more attached than he should have.

Attached?

Face it, he was falling for her in a big way, but that was his problem. She'd been up front with him from the start. She had plans for her future. Career plans. Plans that didn't include him. Tonight proved that, didn't it?

"So what's really going on?" he asked Jacob Powell as he adjusted his headset. "Murphy was pretty cryptic on the phone."

Powell glanced over his shoulder. "I'll let Murphy fill you in. It's big, though. Get ready for some more fireworks."

No one said another word until they were on the ground at Big Sky Bounty Hunters.

WHERE WAS PETROV? Kaitlyn wondered a little while later when Eden led her into the governor's private car. The space was furnished like an office with charcoal leather furniture and a large ebony desk. Seated behind that desk was Peter Gilbert, and he rose when the two women entered the car.

"Welcome aboard," he said warmly. "Eden tells me that you'll be accompanying us on our trip across the state."

"Yes, thanks for having me," Kaitlyn said, still wondering about Petrov. "This is quite a place. I don't think I've ever been inside a private railroad car before."

"First time for everything," Gilbert remarked. "Eden, how about a round of drinks?"

"Certainly." She dropped her wrap and bag, and striding over to a sideboard, began mixing martinis. When she was finished, she handed one to Gilbert, then offered Kaitlyn one.

"Oh, no, thanks. I'm fine."

Eden lifted a brow. "Are you sure? You look a little flustered." She poured herself one and came back over to sit down in the chair where she'd dropped her bag.

"I'm just a little confused about what I'm doing here," Kaitlyn murmured.

"Didn't you say you had some questions you wanted to ask the governor?"

Gilbert's smile was completely disarming. "I would love to stay and answer those questions for you, I really would, but at any moment, Eden will be receiving a call that will require both of us to return to the state capital immediately. The train will get under way with the understanding that we'll catch up with it at the next stop."

Okay, Kaitlyn thought. What was that little speech all about? "I'm afraid I don't understand—"

"No, of course, you don't," Peter Gilbert said. "But you will. You see, Kaitlyn, you've stumbled upon the story of a lifetime. But this time, you really won't live to tell it."

Kaitlyn gasped and staggered back as a memory lashed her like a wave pouring over a ship's prow. "It was you," she said on a breath. "You were up on that mountain with Fowler. You must be the one who arranged to get him out of prison. It had to be someone in power."

Gilbert shrugged. "See? I said you'd put it all together sooner or later."

Kaitlyn put a hand to her mouth. "But... why?"

"Fowler and I go way back. I happen to believe he's right about this country. It's on the wrong track and has been for a very long time. I'm the one who can get going in the right direction again. A savior, if you will. But unfortunately it takes more than vision and ambition to make a dream come true. It also takes a great deal of money."

"Is that why Fowler and his gang killed that ambassador? You're being paid to stop that vote."

"Very good, Kaitlyn," he said approvingly. "But one vote won't stop the resolution from passing. That's why we're being paid to stop the other ambassadors from reaching their destinations as well. It might surprise you to learn that two of them are on board this train even as we speak. They'll never make that secret vote, just as you'll never live to tell your story. The train, you see, is going to meet with a terrible accident. It'll be very tragic and require my undivided attention…right up until the election."

Kaitlyn turned to Eden. "You knew about this?"

"Of course, she knew," Gilbert said. "She and Fowler go back a long way. Don't you, Eden?"

"Oh, my God." The truth hit Kaitlyn with the force of a truck. "You're the one who got Jenny to join the MMFAFA."

"It wasn't hard," Eden said with a shrug. "She wasn't the person you thought she was,

Kaitlyn. She had all this rage and hate bottled up inside her ever since her brother was killed. All I did was give her an outlet."

"With Fowler?" Kaitlyn asked in outrage.

"Boone Fowler happens to be a brilliant man," Eden said matter-of-factly. "I knew the first time my friends and I went to hear him speak back in college that he was someone special. He wanted to change the world, or at least this country, and I wanted to help him."

"By blowing up buildings and killing innocent people?" Kaitlyn demanded.

"We're at war," Eden said softly. "In war, people die. It's called collateral damage. Jenny could have been a valuable asset to us, but then you came back to town, and I knew it was just a matter of time before you'd get her to betray us. You've always had this way about you. And I was right. She came to you, so we had to take care of her."

"Did you kill her?"

"No, that was Fowler. But I made damn sure he knew that he couldn't trust her."

Kaitlyn shook her head. She couldn't believe any of this. "What are you going to do?"

"Just what Peter told you. After we get the phone call, we'll get off the train."

"And then?"

Eden smiled. "You don't want to know."

Kaitlyn's gaze shot to the door, but before she could make a move, Eden whipped out a gun. "Don't do it. I don't want to have to kill you myself, Kaitlyn, but I will if I have to."

"Why?" Kaitlyn asked helplessly. "Why are you doing this?"

"Because I have dreams and ambitions, too," she said coldly. "You understand about that, don't you?"

Her phone rang then, and she and Gilbert exchanged looks.

Eden listened for a moment, hung up the phone and then picked up her bag and wrap. "Time to go."

"Yes, just let me…" Whatever Gilbert was about to say froze on his lips as he lifted a hand to his heart. An astonished expression came over his face as he stared at the drink on his desk, then glanced up. "Eden?" he said on a gasp.

"Sorry, Peter. There's not enough room at

the top for both of us, so I'm afraid I'm the only one getting off this train."

Grabbing his throat now, Gilbert lunged for her, but he lost his balance and pitched forward, landing on the floor with an awful thud.

"So long, Kaitlyn," Eden said softly as she backed through the door.

When she was gone, Kaitlyn flew across the car and tried the door, but Eden had locked it from the outside. Kaitlyn pounded and screamed, but the car was soundproof. No one could hear her.

Realizing her efforts were futile, Kaitlyn checked around the car, trying to find something she could use to bludgeon the door or break out a window.

Then she felt it.

A tiny vibration underneath her feet as the train began to move.

Behind her, Peter Gilbert groaned.

"I GOT IT WRONG," Owen Cook said when Aidan and the others returned to headquarters a little while later.

"What do you mean, you got it wrong?" Aidan demanded.

"Like I said, today's date kept coming up in

all the chatter I'd been monitoring, so I figured it had to be the ball. But I've run across something else in some of the archived messages from those chat rooms. It seems someone's been asking a lot of questions about how to derail a train and make it look like an accident."

"Why an accident?" Aidan asked.

"That we don't know," Murphy said. "But what we need to figure out is which train is their target. Cook and I have been poring over maps and schedules all evening, and I think we've come up with something." He looked up. "Governor Gilbert was scheduled to leave on a whistle-stop tour of the state first thing in the morning, but there's been a schedule change. The train is leaving tonight."

Aidan's heart slammed against his chest as something Kaitlyn had said a few days ago came back to him.

"After that, it's the governor's whistle-stop tour through the state."

"Whistle-stop tour? When did that come about?"

"It's been planned for a while. The train is scheduled to leave sometime after the ball,

and Eden has asked me to ride along in the press car. I can't back out now. I owe her."

The blood in his veins went ice cold. "Kaitlyn is on that train, Colonel." He was sure of it.

"Then you'd better roll," Murphy said.

FOR THE PAST SEVERAL MINUTES, Kaitlyn had been working on the lock with a letter opener she'd found in Gilbert's desk. She hadn't expected to have much luck, but all of a sudden, she felt the tumblers give a little, and she managed to slide the blade between the bolt and the opening. She drew back the door and looked out.

The noise from the tracks and from the wind rushing past the cars was almost deafening. Quickly, Kaitlyn crossed the little platform to the next car and tried to open the door, but it was bolted shut from the *inside*. Eden had thought of everything.

Kaitlyn started to turn back, then froze.

Gilbert was standing in the doorway of his car with a gun pointed at her heart.

He fired, barely missing her, and when he staggered toward her, Kaitlyn glanced around frantically. There was only one way to go.

Up.

To the top of the train.

AS THE CHOPPER DIPPED into the valley, Aidan spotted the train. It was going at a fast clip, and would soon arrive at a series of small towns where a stalled car on a crossing could cause a fatal derailment. Murphy was working the phones now, frantically trying to get the train stopped or, barring that, to make sure that law-enforcement agencies could monitor the crossings.

Of course, the accident might not occur at a crossing. It could happen anywhere along the track...which was the problem. Unless they could get the train stopped, there wouldn't be time to check every square inch of the tracks.

The accident could be devastating. Fatal.

Aidan couldn't think about that now. He had to concentrate on finding Kaitlyn. He didn't have a clear-cut plan in mind except to rappel down to the train and search through every damn car if he had to.

They were flying over the train now, and

through his night-vision goggles, he saw something move on top of one of the cars toward the end of the train. Someone was up there.

"Get lower!" he shouted to Powell.

Powell took the chopper down and turned on the spotlight.

Aidan's heart jumped to his throat. It was Kaitlyn on top of that train!

As he watched her struggle to keep her balance atop the swaying cars, he saw her turn suddenly and drop to her knees. Then he saw why. Someone was on top of the train with her, firing at her at close range.

Throwing off his headset, Aidan flung open the jump door and threw down a rope. Since the train was moving, it was impossible for Powell to establish a hover over the target, which made the maneuver even trickier than usual. But Aidan had done it before, and he could damn sure do it now.

As he started down, a bullet whizzed by him. And then another.

Clinging to the rope with one hand, Aidan opened fire.

He hit the man with the first shot, and with a scream, he fell backward and was whipped by the wind and his momentum from the train.

Kaitlyn was still on her knees. Aidan wasn't even sure if she'd seen him or not.

And then he looked ahead and saw a vehicle across the track in front of them. They were coming up on it fast.

"Jump!" Aidan shouted.

Kaitlyn seemed to rouse from her trance then and saw him.

"Jump!" he screamed again. "Come on!"

Without hesitation, Kaitlyn got to her feet and leaped toward him. He caught her with one hand, and for a terrible moment, he could feel her slip through his fingers.

Then she reached up and grabbed him with both hands as the chopper swung around and the train barreled into the vehicle on the tracks.

Kaitlyn couldn't bear to watch. She closed her eyes and clung to Aidan's hand as the railroad cars began to tip over one by one.

EDEN MCCLAIN GRABBED the laptop and cell phone from the front seat of her Mercedes and carried it with her to the limo that was pulled to the side of the remote, mountainous road in front of her.

Once she was inside, both she and her companion opened their computers and, establishing a satellite linkup, Eden watched as he transferred millions into her Swiss bank account.

When the transaction was completed, she looked up with a smile. "It's been a pleasure doing business with you. I hope our paths will cross again someday."

"I wouldn't be surprised."

She exited the car still smiling and climbed behind the wheel, tossing her laptop and cell phone onto the front seat. Just as she turned the ignition, a cell phone in her purse began to ring.

How odd, she thought. Because *her* cell phone was right there on the seat beside her.

As the limo sped away, the man in the back turned to watch the explosion.

And so it had started.

Chapter Fifteen

One week later

"I just received a briefing from my FBI contact," Murphy told the bounty hunters as they sat grouped around the conference table in the war room. "Several of the victims from the train crash remain in the hospital, but they're all expected to pull through. Which means so far the only fatality is Governor Gilbert."

All eyes turned to Aidan, but he said nothing. It had been an interesting week, not the least of which was the intense interrogation he'd undergone at the hands of the feds. If nothing else, he'd garnered a new respect for the doggedness of the FBI.

"The autopsy substantiated Kaitlyn's claim that the governor had been drugged by his assistant, Eden McClain," Murphy continued.

"The toxicology screen turned up traces of Rohypnol in his bloodstream. She probably figured he'd never regain consciousness. If the train crash didn't kill him, Fowler's men would be on hand to finish the job."

"She double-crossed Gilbert, and then someone double-crossed her," Powell said. "Assuming that the DNA taken from the burned-out car we found matches Eden McClain's."

"I think we can safely assume that it will," Murphy said. "What we have to figure out now is who did the double-crossing and why. Who set her up?"

"You don't think it was Fowler?" someone asked.

Murphy shook his head. "I don't see what he'd have to gain. Remember, Fowler's agenda has always been revolution. Taking back a country he thinks has lost its way. He needs people like Eden McClain working from the inside. No, I don't think Fowler killed her. I think there's another player in the game. Someone who thought she knew too much. Someone with money and power and a willingness to provide the Fowlers of the world with enough guns and bombs to start their own wars. Why else would Fowler get involved in this mess? There has to be something in it for him. And if I'm right…" Murphy's eyes turned steely. "He's even more dangerous than we thought."

"He's still got it in for you," Powell said. "I wouldn't be surprised if he and his men are planning an assault against headquarters even as we speak."

"Which means we've got to find him," Murphy said. "I want that bastard dead or in prison before he hurts someone else. I don't much care which of the two it is."

The men nodded their agreement, and after another few minutes, the meeting concluded and they all filed out of the room. All except Aidan.

Murphy had gone over to stare out the window, but he turned now as Aidan approached. "What is it, Campbell?"

"I just wanted to tell you that I appreciate the way you stood behind me this week. If you hadn't pulled some strings, I'd probably still be in federal detention."

Something glinted in Murphy's eyes. "You shot the damn governor, for God's sake. It's a wonder the feds didn't lock you up and throw away the key."

Aidan shrugged. "He would have killed

Kaitlyn if I hadn't taken him out. You would have done the same thing."

"Damn right I would have." Murphy turned back to the window. "So how did she come through all this?"

"I don't know," Aidan admitted. "I haven't talked to her."

Murphy swung around with a frown. "What do you mean you haven't talked to her?"

Aidan hesitated. "There hasn't been time. We've both been pretty busy with the FBI."

"The feds are through with you now, aren't they? So what's stopping you?"

"It's…complicated."

"It's always complicated, Campbell," Murphy scoffed. "Hell, what fun would it be if it wasn't?"

"Look, you don't understand," Aidan said defensively. "Kaitlyn has done a damn good job reporting this story. She's even had face time on the evening news. She's already had offers from some of the major newspapers around the country, maybe even from the networks. This is an opportunity of a lifetime for her, and I don't want to stand in her way."

Murphy glared at him. "So you're just going to let her walk away?"

"It's too late," Aidan said miserably. "I couldn't stop her even if I wanted to."

"What do you mean?"

"You're not the only one with contacts," Aidan said. "I happen to know that she's booked on a flight to Washington this afternoon. For all I know, she's already left for the airport."

"Then have Powell fire up the Jet Ranger."

Aidan shook his head. "I don't think that's a good idea. She's made up her mind. If she changes it, she knows where I'll be."

"You're a damn fool," Murphy said in disgust.

"THAT'S SOME STORY," Ken commented as he laid aside the latest copy of the *Monitor*. "Escaped convicts, international intrigue, a dirty governor and a childhood friend who betrayed you. It's got Pulitzer written all over. All you have to do is sit back and relax while the job offers keep pouring in."

"I guess so," Kaitlyn said.

Ken sat back in his chair. "So you're off to Washington this afternoon. Tell me you're not really considering taking a job at your old paper. Not after the way they treated you."

"That was as much my fault as theirs," Kaitlyn said with a shrug. "And anyway, I've already made my decision. You know that."

"You're sure about this?"

She nodded. "Absolutely. My mind is made up."

She felt good about her decision, too. It was the right thing to do. Kaitlyn just wished that Aidan would call before she got on the plane this afternoon. She'd like to tell him about her plans before he heard about them from someone else.

But he wasn't going to call. Kaitlyn hadn't heard from him all week. She knew what he was doing, of course. He was stepping aside. Giving her breathing room. Allowing her enough time and space to figure out what she wanted to do with the rest of her life.

Kaitlyn appreciated that. She really did. But it would have been so nice to hear his voice, especially in those trying days after the train crash. But, of course, Aidan had been taken into custody immediately after the shooting so he had hardly been in a position to hold her hand during all those FBI interviews.

It was over now, thank goodness. She and Aidan were both free and clear. And it was time to move on with her life.

So call him.

Not a good idea. Because if she *did* hear his voice, she might never get on that plane this afternoon.

As KAITLYN thumbed through a magazine at a newsstand in the airport a little while later, she was surprised to hear her name being called. She glanced up, her heart thudding, to see Phillip Becker striding toward her.

She tried to damp down her disappointment as she plastered a smile on her face. "Phillip! What are you doing here?"

"I'm flying back to Denver," he said.

"For good?"

"I guess that depends." He gave her a sheepish smile, which took Kaitlyn by surprise again. "I came back to Ponderosa because of a broken engagement," he said. "But my fiancée—ex-fiancée—called a few days ago, and we've started talking. Seems there might be hope for us after all."

"I didn't even know you were engaged," Kaitlyn said.

"No reason that you should. We haven't exactly kept in touch since high school." He hesitated. "I always had a big crush on you, you know."

"You never said anything."

"I guess I thought you were out of my league. You and Eden McClain always seemed so confident and sophisticated. And now when I think about what happened to her…how she betrayed both you and Jenny…" He shook his head. "I never really cared for her, but I'm sorry about what happened to her. I'm sorry for what she tried to do to you, too. Are you okay?"

"I'm getting there."

An announcement came over the speaker and he listened for a moment, then glanced at his watch. "That's me. I've got to run. I saw you standing over here and I wanted to say goodbye in case our paths don't cross again."

"Goodbye, Phillip. And good luck in Denver."

He grinned. "Thanks. To think, I was so

miserable a week ago, and now…" He shook his head. "Amazing how one phone call can change your life."

AFTER PHILLIP LEFT, Kaitlyn took out her cell phone and dialed Aidan's number. "Hi, it's me."

"I know."

It was so good to hear his voice. "I'm at the airport. I'm getting on a plane for Washington in a few minutes, and I just couldn't leave without telling you…" She trailed off, suddenly fighting a lump in her throat that made speech difficult.

"Without telling me what?"

She drew a deep breath. "This would be so much easier if I could see you in person."

"Then turn around."

She whirled.

And there he stood with the phone to his ear. Slowly he hung up and started toward her.

Kaitlyn met him halfway across the room and launched herself into his arms. Wrapping her arms around his neck, she kissed him as fiercely as she had that first day in his Jeep. Maybe more so, because now there was something else in her kiss besides pent-up emotion.

"How did you get past security without a boarding pass?" she asked breathlessly when they finally broke apart.

"I bought a ticket."

He'd bought a ticket just so he could tell her good-bye. How romantic was that?

Kaitlyn stared up at him. "I have to tell you something before I get on that plane."

"I have something I want to say, too." His gaze deepened as his arms tightened around her. "I didn't come here to stop you from leaving, Kaitlyn. I know this is something you have to do."

"But you don't understand—"

He put a finger to her lips. "If you let this opportunity pass you by, you'll always live to regret it. I don't want that for you."

She gave him a tremulous smile. "You don't understand. I've already accepted a job offer back in Ponderosa. I'm only going to Washington because my father's in town. I'll be back on Monday."

He drew back in surprise. "Why didn't you tell me?"

"Why didn't you call me?"

"Because I thought—"

"I needed some space to make a decision?

Well, I've made my decision. I'm staying at the *Monitor*."

Something flared in his eyes, but he was careful to keep his tone neutral. "Kaitlyn, are you sure about this?"

"Of course, I'm sure. I love living in Montana. I always have. And besides—" she gave him a sly smile "—Ken's promised me a raise and a private office. And knowing how much that will get under Allen Cudlow's skin is just icing on the cake."

He grinned. "So you're really coming back."

"Just try and stop me."

They kissed again, and then Kaitlyn pulled back, knowing there was something else she had to tell him before she got on that plane. "I care about you, Aidan. I want to see you when I get back."

"I want to see you, too."

She bit her lip. "I'm not just…a rebound for you?"

He scowled. "A rebound? Whatever gave you that idea?"

"Because you obviously still have feelings for Elena. You may never get over her. I understand that, but I need to know where I stand before I get in too deep."

He traced his knuckles down her face.

"Elena has nothing to do with how I feel about you. I'm falling in love with you, Kaitlyn."

She caught her breath. "I'm falling in love with you, too."

"Then hurry home," he said with a look in his eyes that set her pulse to racing. "Because I'll be right here when you get back."

"I'm counting on that."

She walked away from him then. Presenting her boarding pass to the agent, she turned one last time at the door and waved.

Aidan didn't wave back, but he watched her until she was out of sight down the jetway.

* * * * *

*The action continues next month when
stoic but sexy bounty hunter
Jacob Powell is reunited
with an old flame after a
politician's family is kidnapped.
Don't miss Jessica Andersen's*
BIG SKY BOUNTY HUNTERS
book, BULLSEYE,
only from Harlequin Intrigue!

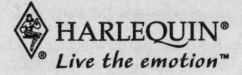
HARLEQUIN®
Live the emotion™

Upbeat,
All-American Romances

flipside
Romantic Comedy

Harlequin Historicals®
Historical,
Romantic Adventure

HARLEQUIN®
INTRIGUE
Romantic Suspense

HARLEQUIN®
HARLEQUIN ROMANCE®
The essence of
modern romance

HARLEQUIN®
Presents
Seduction and passion
guaranteed

HARLEQUIN® *Super*ROMANCE®
Emotional,
Exciting, Unexpected

Temptation
Sassy, Sexy, Seductive!

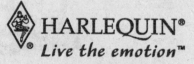